A King Production presents…

Bad Bitches Only

ASSASSINS...

EPISODE 3
(Killing The King)

JOY DEJA KING

This novel is a work of fiction. Any references to real people, events, establishments, or locales are intended only to give the fiction a sense of reality and authenticity. Other names, characters, and incidents occurring in the work are either the product of the author's imagination or are used fictitiously, as those fictionalized events and incidents that involve real persons. Any character that happens to share the name of a person who is an acquaintance of the author, past or present, is purely coincidental and is in no way intended to be an actual account involving that person.

ISBN 10: 1-942217-48-X
ISBN 13: 978-1942217480
Cover concept by Joy Deja King
Cover model: Joy Deja King

Graphic design: www.anitaart79.wixsite.com/bookdesign
Typesetting: Anita J.

Library of Congress Cataloging-in-Publication Data;
A King Production
Assassins...Bad Bitches Only Episode 3/by Joy Deja King
For complete Library of Congress Copyright info visit;
www.joydejaking.com
Twitter @joydejaking

A King Production
P.O. Box 912, Collierville, TN 38027
A King Production and the above portrayal log are trademarks of
A King Production LLC

This Book is Dedicated To My:

Family, Readers and Supporters.
I LOVE you guys so much. Please believe that!!

--Joy Deja King

"Killing The King"

"Chess Is All About Getting The King Into Check. It's About Killing The Father. I Would Say That Chess Has More To Do With The Art Of Murder Than It Does With The Art Of War."

—Arturo Perez-Reverte

A KING PRODUCTION
Bad Bitches Only
ASSASSINS...
EPISODE 3
(Killing The King)
JOY DEJA KING

Chapter One

CHOOSE ME

The plush velvet chairs adorned the second-floor lounge and restaurant area, where customers dined from the menu of food prepared by an executive chef. The ritzy ambiance gave off the aura of a Las Vegas themed supper club. Customers had their choice of the main rooms, the dining area, or private nooks and alcoves scented by candles.

Privilege was a gentleman's club that presented itself as an upscale venue. Entertainers performing in various stages of undress, mingling with customers whose own wardrobe ranged from semiformal to casual. But once the glittery gowns come off and the women stripped down to their G-strings for a $60 lap dance or an impressive performance on the pole, there was no mistaken you were at an Atlanta strip club, just the bad and boujee version. With multiple stages bathed in high-tech lighting, hip hop music blaring from the speakers and champagne flowing, these women were selling a fantasy to the highest bidder and had a slew of men to choose from. But Shiffon had no interest in those other men. Her eyes had remained locked on one.

For the past several weeks, Shiffon had been studying her targets every move, which was no easy task. When she was hired for the job, Faizon had warned her that The King moved in so much silence, he might as well be a ghost. Shiffon figured he was exaggerating but he wasn't. This club was the only place she could track him to. He would show up like clockwork every Wednesday and Thursday. Stay for a few hours, eat dinner, have a few drinks and disappear through a back door. At this point, Shiffon knew she would never get any closer to her mark and it was time to make her move.

"Ladies, ladies, ladies...Get ready to get to work!" Shiffon stood in the middle of the living room floor and announced.

"It's about damn time," Essence smacked. "I was

getting restless. It's only so much retail therapy one can take."

"Speak for yourself," Bailey winked.

"Well, I love a good workout but I was over going to the gym all the time. I'm excited about getting back to work!" Leila grinned, rubbing her hands together. "What's our next assignment? You've been very secretive."

"With good reason. Our new client might be a very dangerous man. I wanted to gather as much information about him as possible before making any moves," Shiffon explained.

"He can't be more dangerous than Dino," Bailey huffed.

"It's ironic you mention Dino because our new client shares the same occupation as your now deceased boyfriend. Except he's much higher on the totem pole." Shiffon stated.

"How much higher?" Bailey was curious to know.

"They call him The King. So on the streets, about as high as you can get without being the head of a cartel," she remarked. "Everyone in this room knows, I'm not about that bullshit so let me be clear. This might get very ugly." Shiffon made eye contact with each of the women before continuing. "If any of you would prefer to sit out this particular job, I don't have a problem with that."

"How much is it paying?" Essence questioned.

"It pays extremely well but all money ain't good

money. I enjoy what I do, so I'm willing to take the risks but I can't ask you all to do what I do," Shiffon clarified.

"Look, when I asked to join Bad Bitches Only, I knew you all weren't in the kitchen baking cookies," Leila popped. "We're assassins. It is what it is. I'm in."

"Me too," Bailey nodded.

"Shit...wit' all the money I've been spending lately, I'm definitely in!" Essence added.

"Since we all onboard, let's deal with the next issue..." Shiffon exhaled.

"Which is?" Bailey asked.

"Which one of you lovely ladies will be bait for our target. Any volunteers?" Shiffon questioned. "Oh wow! I wasn't expecting all three of you to raise your hands."

"We want to be team players," Leila smiled.

"That's great. I'm just surprised you all would agree to be bait for a man you've never seen before. Especially you, Essence. You can be so picky when it comes to men." Shiffon eyed her friend with wariness.

"Okay...you got me!" Essence folded her arms. "The other day I was in your bedroom looking for something and I noticed a folder that had potential client written on it. I decided to take a peek and saw pictures of a fine ass nigga!" She blurted.

"I knew yo' ass volunteered way too quickly. And let me guess. You shared those pics with the other two musketeers," Shiffon cracked, eyeing Bailey and Leila.

"Fine! We're guilty too," Bailey shrugged. "Now

that you know we're all more than happy to play seductress, how will you decide who to use?"

"I guess the old fashioned way. Each of you write your name down. Put it in a jar and whichever name I choose is the winner," Shiffon reasoned.

Shiffon grabbed a notepad from the kitchen counter and tore off three pieces of paper. She handed one to each of the women and they began writing their name down.

"Where's yours?" Leila asked, handing Shiffon her folded paper.

"Oh, I'm not participating. I want to focus my attention on the most important part...the murder." Shiffon stated, taking the other two folded papers and tossing all three in a vase on the coffee table.

"Good! That makes my odds of winning even better," Essence laughed.

"Girl, I hope you do win. Maybe you can finally get some dick," Shiffon joked, pausing for a few seconds once she opened the paper.

"Say the name!" The three ladies shouted simultaneously, dying to know which one of them would be trying to cozy up to the handsome kingpin.

"It's you, Bailey," Shiffon sighed holding up the paper.

"Yes!" Bailey clapped her hands excitedly, while Essence and Leila sulked with disappointment.

"Bailey, are you sure you're up to this?" Shiffon felt the need to ask.

"Of course I am! Why would you even ask me that?" she questioned becoming defensive.

"What happened with Dino wasn't that long ago. You can't blame me for having doubts that you're ready for this."

"Why did you even put my name in the mix, if you think I'm so weak, Shiffon?!" Bailey balked.

"I don't think you're weak," she told her cousin. "But I'd be lying if I didn't say I'm concerned," Shiffon admitted.

"Is the job mine or not?" Bailey wanted to know.

"I chose your name, so the answer is yes," Shiffon nodded.

"Wonderful," Bailey said with defiance. "Now tell me what I need to do to help you kill The King."

Chapter Two

CATTITUDE

Shiffon wasted no time throwing Bailey straight into the lion's den. As if with a snap of the finger, she went from sitting on the sofa in the living room to the VIP section of Privilege Gentleman's Club, making small talk with a patron.

"I come here pretty often during the week but I've never seen you. Do you usually work on the weekends?" the well-dressed older man asked Bailey.

"Actually I'm new. This is my very first night," she smiled sweetly.

"Really. You should do well here. You caught my attention," he winked, taking another sip of his drink.

"I think I'm ready for that lap dance now."

Fuck! This is what my ass get for being so damn thirsty. I thought this gig would only require me to put on some cute clothes and flirt with a sexy nigga. I had no idea it would require me to prance around half naked, grinding to some music. Thank goodness I'm used to struttin' around in high heels, Bailey thought to herself unzipping her gown. *Here goes nothing.*

When the beat dropped to **Wish Wish**, Bailey closed her eyes to help her concentrate. She began to shake her ass like she was Diamond in the movie Players Club, struggling to make enough money to pay for her college education. Luckily she knew how to synchronize her movements to the music glaring from the speakers, simply swaying her hips to the track. Bailey turned to the side, arching her back, highlighting her silhouette for the customer. She was taking deep breaths, trying to calm her nerves. As being basically naked on full display was causing her more anxiety than she expected. But when Bailey felt the touch of cold hands fondling her flesh, anxiety turned to annoyance. She opened her eyes ready to curse the customer out but she froze.

Oh fuck...that's him...The King, Bailey thought to herself locking eyes with her target. *I could never forget the face of a man that fine.* He was sitting directly across from their table in a booth with a couple other men. His stare was intense but brief. He went right back to talking to the dudes at his booth, leaving Bailey feeling disappointed.

"Pretty girl, why you stopping?" the man questioned, gripping Bailey's waist.

"You do know there's a no touching policy here," she snapped, pushing his hand away.

"For the right price, policies don't matter," he retorted, flashing a wad of cash.

This nigga can't be serious, Bailey rolled her eyes, prepared to tell the man to take that cash and shove it up his ass. Then she heard Shiffon's voice screaming in her head.

Girl, you better get that attitude in check. You have a job to do and that means playing your role. So wipe that frown off your face and smile.

"True but maybe next time," Bailey teased, gliding her ballerina pink coffin nail with diamond accents over his bottom lip. "The name you just heard over the speakers is me. It's my turn to take the stage," she grinned, grabbing her dress.

Bailey rushed off relieved to get away from her touchy, feely customer, although she wasn't looking forward to taking the stage for the first time. As she rushed to take her position, Bailey noticed two women standing by a table, side eyeing her.

"Watch where you going!" The stripper who just finished her set snapped at Bailey, as she was coming down the stairs.

"I suggest you do the same!" Bailey barked back, slightly nudging the woman with her shoulder when they passed each other.

These hoes been acting shady as hell since I got here. They need to let me do my job and stay the fuck out my way, Bailey thought to herself as Rihanna's **Pour It Up** echoed through the speakers. The seductive beat had Bailey slithering across the stage and then seamlessly morphing her body around the stripper pole. Maybe it was the nasty glares that greeted her from some of the other dancers before taking the stage or her desire to get the man still only known to her as The King, attention but Bailey was putting on quite the show. No one would even guess she was a newbie at this. To take it a step further, she decided to implement some of the skills she learned while being a high school cheerleader. Once Bailey slid down and did a full fledge split, thrusting her hips slow but steady, she had captured the attention of everyone in the room.

Yes Bitch, you is killin' it!! Bailey smiled to herself while maintaining her stripper siren pose. A group of men had gathered flashing nothing but cash. Bailey was taking her role as a stripper seriously and sashayed her ass over to collect them funds. Little did she know the catty chicks in the corner whose facial expressions were full of disapproval, criticism and scorn had conspired...literally for her downfall. Before the previous dancer left the stage, she poured a small amount of baby oil a few feet away from the edge of the stage. Talk about slippery when wet. The instant Bailey's six inch heels touched the spot, her legs went flying up, propelling her entire body off the stage. Luckily one of the men who had gathered near the stage was close enough to help break Bailey's fall. Instead of slamming into the floor at full speed, his bit of padding provided enough support to only slightly bruise her upper thigh instead of busting her ass.

"I told you to watch where you going. You shoulda took my advice." The stripper stopped in front of Bailey, taunting her.

"Fuck you!" Bailey shouted, ready to jump on the girl but when she tried to stand up, she screamed out in pain.

"Let me help you up," the man who kept Bailey from crashing to the floor offered. He carried her over to the chair and sat her down.

"Thank you but I'm fine now," Bailey sighed, zooming in on her bruise to further inspect. When she glanced up, Bailey noticed the same group of catty chicks staring at her and laughing.

Them bitches better be lucky I ain't in no condition to fight cause I would drag they asses. Not giving a fuck that I'm outnumbered, Bailey fumed to herself. *They might be giggling and shit at my expense right now but I'll have the last laugh...bet.*

"Looks like the new girl ain't gonna get past the initiation," Malcom commented to The King, as they both stood on the top balcony of the club staring down.

"Yeah, after that fall, I doubt she'll be back. The

stripper life ain't for everybody."

"It's too bad. Shawty looked fuckin' good on that stage."

The King nodded his head. "I agree."

Chapter Three

DESTINED TO FAIL

"Has either of you spoken to Bailey today?" Shiffon asked, looking in the refrigerator trying to decide what she was going to eat for lunch.

"Nope," Essence answered. "I just asked Leila the same thing. She must've gotten in really late."

"Yeah because I didn't hear her when she came in and I was asleep on the couch. And she hasn't come out her bedroom yet," Leila added.

"Speaking of couches, how long are you going to be sleeping on ours?" Essence smacked.

"Until it becomes a problem and Shiffon said it wasn't."

"Well Shiffon doesn't live here by herself," Essence cracked.

"Bailey doesn't mind either. The only person complaining is you," Leila fussed.

"Can we not do this today," Shiffon closed the refrigerator, deciding to eat out instead. "Essence, we already discussed this. Leila is trying to save up her money to find her own place. Until then, she's staying here with us. Unless you want to dig into your piggybank and give her the money," Shiffon mocked.

"I don't have no money to give right now but why can't she go get a roommate like every other struggling chick in Atlanta be doing."

"First of all Essence, you can stop talkin' about me like I ain't standing right here!" Leila exclaimed.

Shiffon put her hand up as soon as she saw Essence open her mouth ready to start yapping.

"Listen, I already told you because of the business we're in, I didn't want Leila getting a roommate," Shiffon reminded Essence. "We don't need no nosey broads all in our shit. Until she can afford to get a nice apartment in a safe neighborhood then Leila will be staying here. I thought the two of you had worked out whatever differences you had," she huffed.

"I don't have a problem with Essence. I guess she still ain't gettin' no dick and blame me for it." Leila got the last jab before Bailey entered the kitchen.

"Good afternoon ladies," Bailey said getting some ibuprofen from the kitchen cabinet.

"I was beginning to think you had turned into a vampire and we wouldn't see you until the sun went down," Shiffon joked. "I guess you had a long night."

"You have no idea." Bailey shook her head, washing down the pills with some water. "Let's start with this bruise on my thigh," she said lifting up her bathrobe flashing the women.

"What happened?!" Leila walked over to Bailey to examine the garish purple splotches that was roughly the size of a fist.

"That looks terrible!" Essence gasped.

"Trust me it could be a lot worse," Bailey shrugged.

"It does look pretty bad and very painful," Shiffon admitted. "Now I understand why you've been in bed all day. I think you should stay off your feet for a few days. Leila or Essence can go in your place and work tonight at the club."

"I'll go!" Leila quickly volunteered.

"I got this! I'll go in Bailey's place. I know a thing or two about strip clubs. My previous roommate was a top earner at one and schooled me on how to work your way around the club," Essence explained.

"Thanks but neither of you will be going because I'll be showing up for work tonight," Bailey stated firmly. "Ain't no bitter bitches gon' run me out the club. I can hold my own."

"Is that base I hear in your voice. Did my cousin

grow some balls," Shiffon smirked.

"You damn right. Who knew the strip club was such a jungle and I ain't talking about the thirsty men neither. If you can survive those catty women, then you can survive just about anything." Bailey rolled her eyes, replaying the tumble she took from last night.

"Didn't nobody but them paws on you did they?" Essence wanted to know.

"Yeah cause if they did, I'll catch them outside. They won't even know you had anything to do with it," Shiffon promised.

"I know you have my back, Shiffon," Bailey grinned. "If I need you to step in, I'll let you know. For now, I'm focused on getting at our target."

"So did you even make contact with The King and do you know his real name yet?" Essence questioned.

"Yes and no," Bailey replied. "Yes, I did make eye contact with The King and no I don't know his real name yet. We didn't have a chance to talk but hopefully tonight that will change."

"But can you even dance with that bruise?" Shiffon was concerned.

"It looks more painful than what it really is. Last night it was terrible but today not so bad. I took the ibuprofen to eliminate any discomfort, so I'll be able to dance just fine. I'll put some makeup on to cover the bruise and I'll be as good as new," Bailey smiled. "No one will even remember I almost busted my ass last night."

"I'm loving this optimistic attitude of yours. I'm very proud of you Bailey," Shiffon winked. "Now if you ladies excuse me, I have some errands to run. Essence and Leila, follow Bailey's lead and behave," she said eyeing the two women. "Call me if you need me."

Shiffon hurried out, wanting to leave before any bickering started. She decided if Essence and Leila didn't stop arguing, she was going to throw them in the ring and let them fight it out like two boxers.

"Damn Bailey, with this new attitude of yours, I may not be able to call you our little princess anymore," Essence commented after Shiffon left.

"Like I told you, the princess died in me after my nightmare with Dino. I had no choice but to learn to protect myself."

"I feel you. Going through that sort of trauma would change anybody. A lot of women would be more afraid and shy away from any sort of danger, which is understandable," Essence said.

"Dare I say, I agree with Essence. But it seems to have had the opposite effect on you, Bailey. It's made you a lot stronger," Leila nodded.

"It's not just about Dino. I know Shiffon has major concerns about me doing this job. She doesn't think I'm cut out for it. I'm determined to prove her wrong. I want my cousin to see that I'm a valuable asset to Bad Bitches Only. Not some charity case she needs to protect like I'm a baby."

"Shiffon doesn't see you as a baby. You're her little

cousin. Of course she's protective of you," Essence reasoned.

"Give me a break. I'm only a few years younger than her," Bailey protested.

"It doesn't matter, she's still protective of you," Essence continued.

"Well it matters to me. After I bring down The King, Shiffon will finally have to see me as her equal," Bailey reasoned. "Now excuse me. I have to go get ready for work."

"I think that went well," Leila said getting up from the kitchen table.

"Of course you would," Essence moaned begrudgingly. "Personally, I think it went terrible."
"Why do you say that?"

"I'm afraid Bailey is setting herself up to fail. She can't compete with Shiffon and she shouldn't try. They're cut from different cloths."

"I don't think Bailey is trying to compete with Shiffon. I just think she wants her cousin's approval. What's wrong with that?" Leila asked.

"Why would you want something that's impossible to get. Compete...get her approval...whatever it's the same damn thing as far as I'm concerned. Either way, Bailey won't get it. Wait and see. We just better hope, she doesn't ruin this gig in the process. Essence grabbed her drink and headed to her bedroom leaving Leila to wonder if she was right and Bailey was destined to fail

Chapter Four

STEPPING STONE

Bailey was right back at it, in Privilege shaking her ass and collecting them coins. She made sure to hustle extra hard just to piss off them hoes who tried to run her off. With the architectural LED lighting in the club and some Dermablend, Bailey's unappealing bruise was nonexistent. And any inhibitions she had about being naked around complete strangers seemed to disappear within the last twenty-four hours. She was dressing and undressing with ease.

"I didn't think you would show up here tonight." The deep, smooth voice spoke in Bailey's ear.

"Why the fuck not. I work here." Bailey stated

coolly, turning around to see who had startled her. She was welcomed by the darkest eyes she had ever seen. The sort that pulled you all the way in but sent a chill of fear down your spine.

"True but after that fall you took last night, I figured you was done here." His intense stare remained steady.

"You figured wrong," Bailey said, folding the money she'd just collected over the garter belt on her thigh, securing it with a rubber band.

"It's rare but on occasion I've been wrong," he conceded, then skipping straight into introducing himself. "Rashan and yours? Not yo' stripper name either."

"Ayana," Bailey replied, almost forgetting the new identity Shiffon supplied her with.

"Ayana, come sit with me."

"I can't. It's my turn to hit the stage."

"The stage can wait."

"Not if I wanna keep my job and I need the money," she said, not wanting to come across as too eager to follow his lead. One thing Shiffon always stressed to her was a man enjoys a little bit of a chase. She would say; only time a nigga looking for an easy chick, is when he just need a bitch to ride his dick right quick. As Bailey walked away, Rashan reached out placing his hand on her wrist.

"I own this place. So like I said, the stage can wait."

"Well excuse me." Bailey's tone was haughty yet demure. "I would be foolish to disrespect my boss."

A hint of a smile danced on her lips as she surveyed Rashan's face, thinking to herself, her little game had paid off. Bailey had caught the eye and made contact with The King.

"Look who the new bitch is talking to," Dalia smacked to Evte. "After that tumble she took on the stage, I was certain she wouldn't show her face here tonight."

"Well you shoulda poured more baby oil on the stage to make sure she broke a leg," Evte quipped.

Dalia cut her eyes at Evte before directing her attention back on Rashan. "Do you think he's interested in her?" she questioned. "I mean he rarely says two words to the strippers who work at this club."

"It's hard to tell with Rashan. She's the new girl and she did bust her ass. He might wanna make sure she's not gonna file a lawsuit. He is a businessman," Evte shrugged.

"Maybe but I don't like it," Dalia sneered.

"What is yo' issue wit' her?" Evte questioned while adjusting her G-string before taking the stage. "She cute an all and..."

"If you implying I'm jealous, you wrong!" Dalia snapped, cutting Evte off.

"Then what?"

"Something about her don't feel right. She shows up out the blue and scores a job here. Now she all up in Rashan's face."

"It look like he all up in her face to me," Evte

21

cracked. "We can talk about this later. I gotta hit the stage."

"I hope yo' dumbass fall," Dalia mumbled under her breath when Evte walked away. *I don't give a fuck what you say Evte, that chick up to something. If she think she gonna schmooze up to the boss and become the queen of this club, she out her muthafuckin' mind. The only queen in this bitch is me,* Dalia said to herself, as she began plotting on how to get rid of who she considered to be her rival.

"Alex, I was surprised when I got your phone call," Shiffon remarked when she entered his condo. "I didn't think you would be needing my services again so soon." "Have a seat, Shiffon. Can I get you anything to drink?" he offered.

"No I'm good," she said taking in the awe-inspiring views of the southern skyline. Although it would seem out of reach to the average person, Shiffon visualized being able to afford to live in such luxury one day, glancing down at the heated Onyx marble floors in the entry hall before sitting down. "So what can I do for you?"

"Actually it's not for me but someone I've done business with in the past," Alex explained. "I was very pleased with how you handled the Enzo situation."

"Thank you but I was very surprised to hear about

his accidental drug overdose. Of course I didn't know him personally but I never got the impression he was a hardcore drug user."

"Shiffon, I think we both know there was nothing accidental about Enzo's death. I don't take too kindly to people playing me."

"Even people that make you millions and millions of dollars?"

"Have you ever heard the saying, a person is worth more dead than alive. That especially applies to music artists that die at the height of their career and have hundreds of never released songs."

"Wait, so you had Enzo record a ton of new music before he died?"

"I'm a businessman, so of course I did," Alex nodded. "I flew him to Hawaii on a private jet, where he stayed for a month at a fully staffed estate, top of the line studio, best producers and his closest friends. Enzo recorded enough songs that I can at least put out six platinum albums," he stated confidently.

"Wow, impressive, Alex. Talk about premeditation of murder."

"They don't call me a shrewd businessman for nothing. But enough about Enzo. I asked you to come over because a young nigga I've done business with, needs a particular sort of job done and he asked if I could recommend anyone. The first person I thought about is you. Now the job is in Philly. Will that be a problem for you?" Alex questioned.

"Not at all. I actually lived in Philly for a period of time."

"Good, so you should know your way around."

"I do. What kind of job is this? I mean I know murder must be involved."

"I'll let Caleb give you all the details."

"I'm assuming Caleb is the person who's hiring me?" Shiffon wanted to make sure.

"Yes. He's a major mover in the drug game. Whatever he needs you to do, it'll be dangerous. He won't have you chasing down a bunch of clout chasing broads like I did. I like you and respect you, so I wanted to be upfront. There's no sense in you meeting with Caleb if this ain't something you wanna touch."

"I always appreciate your candor, Alex. But for the right price, I have no issue touching danger."

"Trust me, money won't be an issue. If the job is done right, Caleb will pay whatever price. So should I link the two of you up?"

"Do you even have to ask. If you vouching for him, of course link us up." Shiffon paused. "There is one issue."

"What's that?"

"I'm in the middle of another case right now, so I can't go to Philly. Can your guy come to Atlanta for us to meet and discuss the details?"

"That shouldn't be a problem. I'll set it up and be in touch."

"Sounds like a plan," Shiffon said glancing down

at her watch. "I hate to chat and run but I do have some other business to tend to," she said standing up.

"I understand," Alex smiled. "It's always good to see you and I'll be in touch," he said walking Shiffon to the door.

"Looking forward to it." And Shiffon was. This would be Bad Bitches Only first job without Binky being the middleman, which meant all the money would be going to them. They wouldn't have to share a cut of the profit with him. Shiffon hoped this would the first of many more to come.

Chapter Five

INCHING CLOSER

When Bailey opened her eyes, she was initially consumed with regret. She woke up in Rashan's bed. *I can't believe I fucked this nigga! I knew I shouldn't have had all those glasses of champagne. The bubbly always makes me so damn tipsy,* she thought to herself. It wasn't until Bailey glanced down and realized she wasn't naked that a sigh of relief came over her. She was wearing her bra, panties and one of Rashan's t-shirts.

"Good afternoon. You finally decided to wake up."

Rashan entered the bedroom, opening the window blinds via remote by flipping a light switch. Allowing in a room full of natural sunlight.

"Did you say afternoon?! Fuck! I have to be to work in a few hours. I knew I should've declined your invitation to come over for drinks."

"Don't worry. I told Malcom you won't be coming in for work today."

"Are you sure that's a good idea? I mean I just started working there," Bailey said, sitting up in the bed.

"You worry too much. Now go get dressed, we going out." Rashan wasn't giving Bailey a choice, he was making a demand.

"Where are we going?" she asked.

"I'll let you know when we get in the car.

"Is it okay if I take a shower first?"

"Not a problem but don't take too long. I'm not a patient man."

"Then I'll make it quick." Bailey grabbed her clothes off the chair, giving Rashan a half smile before disappearing into the bathroom.

"Has anyone seen Bailey? We were supposed to go to the nail salon today before she went to work?" Leila asked Shiffon and Essence who were sitting on the outside patio having drinks.

"I assumed she was still in her room sleeping from a long night at the club," Shiffon said lowering her sunglasses.

"No. I checked her bedroom and her bed is made up." Leila told them.

"I've been up since early this morning and I haven't seen Bailey. If her bed is made up, that means she didn't come home last night," Essence told them with panic in her voice.

"Both of you calm down," Shiffon said, not wanting to think the worse. "Let me try calling her."

"I've already tried calling her and I left a voice-mail," Leila said nervously.

"Maybe she left her phone in the car, let's try calling her again." Shiffon reached for her iPhone. "Bailey just sent me a text message," she said, feeling relieved.

"What did she say?!" Leila and Essence asked simultaneously.

"She's with Rashan."

"Who the fuck is Rashan?" Essence frowned.

"The King," she revealed. A surge of nervous excitement shot through Shiffon's body. "This is good... this is really good. "Thank goodness I already got the apartment set up for her. Let me text Bailey the address and tell her where I left the key," she said, while texting her cousin back.

"You got an apartment for Bailey...and if so why can't Leila live there? She needs a place to stay,"

Essence added, side eyeing Leila.

"Because the apartment is strictly for business. I didn't think it would happen this soon but I wanted to make sure Bailey had a place to take The King...I mean Rashan, once they started seeing each other. We surly couldn't have her bringing him here," Shiffon rationalized.

"Shiffon, you continue to impress me. You're always thinking one step ahead," Leila smiled.

"Well, that's why I'm the boss. And when you're dealing with a man like Rashan, you better be at least one step ahead, or you can very easily end up dead. Bailey almost loss her life once before because I wasn't thorough. I won't take that chance again," Shiffon promised.

"Are you going to tell me where your driver's taking us?" Bailey asked, glancing out the backseat passenger window.

"Phipps Plaza," Rashan said, not taking his eyes off his phone.

"You don't look like you need to do anymore shopping," Bailey joked but she was serious.

Rashan had impeccable taste. He dressed as if headed to a laidback boardroom meeting instead of pushing a massive quantity of drugs to the streets. From his Santoni loafers, to his dark navy Italian-made Valentino cotton & silk pants, paired with a white fitted V-neck Our Legacy t-shirt, which accented his broad, muscular frame. His pecs were full and well defined with wide lats that only added to his perfect V shaped frame and slender torso. Rashan's back muscles were even visible whenever he stretched any part of his upper body. The only obscene bling he wore was a Piaget Altiplano tourbillon watch. Case in 18k white gold set with 265 brilliant-cut diamonds and 48 baguette-cut diamonds. Dial set with 511 brilliant-cut diamonds, plus the crown set and buckle set had diamonds too. His watch was literally flooded and blinding you with diamonds. The man was fine, rich, powerful and he knew it.

"This stop to Phipps is for you. I'm sure you don't wanna walk around all day in the same clothes you had on last night." Rashan stated, continuing to keep his eyes directed on his phone.

Bailey glanced down at the white soft brushed-back fleece cropped hoodie with matching jogger pants. Her Nike fit was street-chic, cozy and comfortable. She felt it was the perfect attire for when you're headed to work at a strip club, where you'd be half-naked most of the night. Now she was feeling a bit self-conscious.

I guess my ultra-comfy look isn't that appealing to Rashan. I mean riding in the back of a chauffeured driven luxury SUV with a drug kingpin, I suppose my outfit could be a little cuter, Bailey thought to herself staring over at Rashan, who seemed to get better looking with each passing minute.

"Of course I don't wanna wear the same clothes I had on yesterday but it's not like I planned on spending the night with you."

"I know that's why I'm taking you shopping."

"I don't want you to feel obligated to take me shopping because I didn't bring a change of clothes. Does my gear look that bad to you?" Bailey asked, becoming offended.

"I don't ever feel obligated to anybody. After I make some stops, we're having dinner and I want you to look good. Nothing more...nothing less."

Bailey was struggling to get a read on Rashan. She sat back in her seat and started replaying their conversation from last night, before going back to his crib and getting drunk.

"So what do you wanna talk about?" Bailey asked with a flirtatious attitude, crossing her legs and leaning forward.

"I'm not one of yo' customers. You don't have to try to work me. I just wanna get to know you a lil' better. You are working in my club."

"True. Do you take an interest in everyone that works at your club?" Bailey wanted to know.

"Yeah I do."

"And here I thought I was special."

"Are you...are you special? Or are you just another stripper working in the club?"

Rashan's question was so bold and unexpected, Bailey found herself unwittingly answering truthfully.

"I used to think I was special but now I'm not so sure. Honestly, I don't feel special at all." A glimpse into Bailey's raw vulnerability made her even more appealing to Rashan.

"I'm about to leave. Go get your stuff. You're coming with me." Rashan stood up and started to walk off, as if he was certain Bailey would follow. And as he expected, she did.

"We're here." Rashan announced, shaking Bailey out of her thoughts. It didn't matter because her reminiscing over their initial conversation, did nothing to help her better understand the man she was hired to kill.

Chapter Six

ALL YOU GET IS ONE SHOT

"Girl, I saw this bad ass dress I'ma wear to that party tonight," Dalia told her friend Tinaye as they pulled up to Phipps Plaza.

"I already know what I'm wearing and that shit sexy as fuck. All I need to do is get me some shoes," Tinaye said, pulling down the visor. "I gotta make sure I look cute," she winked in the mirror. "You know plenty of rich niggas be up in here," Tinaye giggled putting on some more lip gloss. "My lips gotta be poppin.'"

"Bitch, I'm just so muthafuckin' happy I ain't gotta

work tonight. We shakin' our ass all night long…no stripper pole needed," Dalia joked, grabbing her purse. She stepped out the car but then hesitated.

"Something wrong wit' yo' legs? Why you stopping?" Tinaye cracked.

"That lowdown hussy!" Dalia fumed getting back in the car and slamming the door.

"What tha fuck got you in yo' feelings?!" Tinaye wanted to know. Dalia seemed to be in a trance and quickly realized she was staring at two men and a woman exiting the mall. One of the men was solid, big and had a strong firm body, dressed in all black. He was walking a few feet ahead and appeared to be a bodyguard.

"Yo how in the fuck did this bitch manage to get that nigga! And she got on that dusty ass jogging suite she wore last night to work," Dalia hissed.

"Girl, you know that fine ass nigga walking wit' that chick?!

"Yeah I know him!" Dalia shouted. "You see all those shopping bags that hoe carrying," she huffed. "I can't believe he took her ass shopping."

"Bitch! Don't tell me that Rolls-Royce Cullinan the valet just pulled up in, is his shit!" Now Tinaye was feeling salty. "Them SUV's start at $330,000 a pop!"

"Sholl is and that's just one of his whips. That nigga own the strip club I work at and from what I hear, got his hands in a bunch of other shit too. I don't know what he see in her," Dalia complained, playing with her twenty inch body wave weave.

"Girl, don't trip off that broad. Yeah he fine and rich but we in the A. There's more like him," Tinaye shrugged. "If we get out this fuckin' hot ass car and go in the mall, we might can find us one or maybe even two just like him."

Dalia heard what her friend was saying but she wasn't listening. She was too fixated on Bailey and Rashan. She was sizing Bailey up from her top knot bun, down to her teal tint Nike Air VaporMax shoes. Her casual, bare face look was in complete contrast to the heavy makeup, wild hair and scantily dresses Bailey pranced around the club in.

I been working at Privilege for over two years and that nigga Rashan ain't done so much as brushed up against my ass. This heffa been shakin' her tits in the club for less than a week and she parading around these streets wit' our boss. Like why...what does he see in her? Let me find out Rashan falling for that sweet and innocent look she going for today. She might got him fooled but not me. Ain't no hoe who can grind on a pole like she did the other night, is that innocent. We all got secrets and I'ma find out what hers are, Daila said to herself.

Shiffon pulled up to the run down house in Grove Park and immediately regretted agreeing to meet Faizon there. Grove Park was in northwest Atlanta, inside the perimeter neighborhood bounded by Center Hill on the west. Dixie Hills, West Lake, and Hunter Hills on the south. Bankhead on the east. Almond Park, West Highlands and Rockdale to the north. Grove Park was one, if not the worst neighborhoods in Atlanta and Shiffon was dead in the center of it.

"Out of all the places we could've met, is there a reason you insisted on me coming here?" Shiffon asked, walking up on Faizon, who was standing outside smoking a cigarette.

"This wasn't my first choice," he said, tossing his cigarette on the ground and stepping on it to put it out. "I got held up and wasn't sure when I'd be done here. But I needed to speak wit' you and no it couldn't wait," Faizon made clear before Shiffon could ask.

"So what's up?" Shiffon questioned, scanning the area. She was feeling uneasy. Every house on the street, besides maybe two or three appeared to be boarded up and abandoned, yet cars were steadily driving up and down the street. "You gotta crackhouse over here or something."

"Damn sure do," Faizon chuckled. "Come on inside so we can continue our conversation."

Once inside the cramped two bedroom home, Shiffon wanted to immediately turn around and get the hell out. "What type of bullshit is this? I don't need to be here seeing this shit," Shiffon gasped.

"What's the problem? In the line of work you in,

this should be nothing to you," Faizon casually replied. Shiffon glanced back over to the two men who were each hogtied and chained to a chair in the kitchen. Both were badly beaten and bloody with duct tape covering their mouths.

"Tech, this the young lady I was telling you about," Faizon said to his worker who was holding a machete in one hand and a crowbar in the other.

"Shiiiiit, when did hired killers start lookin' like that! I know niggas be shook when they find out yo' pretty ass will literally kill a muthafucka," Tech clowned.

Man what tha fuck in the haunted house hell did I step into. This nigga holding a machete like he Jason from Friday the 13th. If Faizon hadn't already given me a large deposit and Bad Bitches Only wasn't in desperate need of the money, I would seriously walk away from this foolishness. But since that ain't an option, let me find out what the fuck Faizon want so I can get outta here, Shiffon thought to herself.

"Listen, I'm already running late for a meeting with another client," Shiffon lied and said.

"Are they paying you as much as me? If not, then they can wait."

"They're actually paying me more but even if they weren't, I treat all my clients with the same level of professionalism." Shiffon stated, becoming distracted when she realized one of the men who was being tortured, was pissing on himself.

"That's why I fuck wit' you, Shiffon. Cause I respect how you conduct yo' business," Faizon nodded with approval.

"Thank you. Now can you tell me what's so urgent." Shiffon pressed, ready to go.

"You see those two men over there..." Faizon pointed his index finger in their direction as if anyone could miss the bloody bodies, who appeared to be on the brink of death.

"Yes, what about them?" Shiffon wanted Faizon to hurry up and get to the fuckin' point.

"They work for The King. You know, the man I hired you to kill."

"You mean Rashan. This is my first opportunity to share that bit of info with you," Shiffon explained.

"Good to know. That's more information I was able to get outta the two of them." Faizon this time nodded his head in the direction of his captives. "I guess that means you finally makin' progress."

"We are but you knew this assignment would require a lot of time. The information you gave me on Rashan was limited. He's indeed a hard man to gain access to but we're making it work."

"Excellent cause I need that nigga gone. Them two punk asses opened shop near one of my blocks. What was once my most profitable location has now become my lowest money maker. I sent them mutha-fuckers warning shots to close shop or else but they musta thought a nigga was joking. Now the joke on them." Faizon gave a devilish grin, proud of what he considered to be a major accomplishment.

"Faizon man, these niggas ain't gon' tell us shit! At this point, I'm tired of torturing they asses," Tech grumbled. "What tha fuck you want me to do?"

"Lullaby they asses," Faizon shrugged.

Shiffon didn't even have a chance to protest. She would've preferred Tech did his killing once she was out the door. Instead all she saw was brains splattered on the refrigerator, cabinets and every other spot in the kitchen. He reached in the back of his pants for the gun with such quickness, Shiffon had no time to turn away so she wouldn't have to witness the bloodshed.

Shiffon wanted to curse Faizon the fuck out but she kept her cool. *This nigga is a piece of work. He wanted me to see his henchman murder Rashan's workers. Is this a fuckin' test or is this muthafucka tryna warn me that this will happen to me and my crew, if we don't serve him up a dead Rashan. Yo it's true, all money ain't good money,* Shiffon said to herself.

"I wish I could stay and help yo' man Tech clean up the mess he just made but I really gotta go," Shiffon winked, maintaining her composure.

"Not so fast." Faizon stepped forward reducing the space between them. "If you have a name for me, then it means you're able to get to the nigga."

"Yes one of my girl's has made contact but I don't have all the details yet. I should have more for you by tomorrow. I'll keep you updated but right now, I really need to go."

"A'ight but remember one thing, Shiffon."

"What's that?"

"If you aim at The King, make sure you kill his ass the first time, cause you won't get a second chance," Faizon warned.

Chapter Seven

DANCE WITH DANGER

"You clean up nicely," Rashan remarked as he and Bailey were having dinner at Restaurant Eugene in Buckhead. They were seated at a U-shaped booth against the wall, enjoying the five-course chef tasting menu with wine pairings. The fine dining establishment was small, intimate, romantic with an air of sophistication. The kind of place that could easily make a woman feel like she was in love, even if it was actually only lust.

"Thank you but you've seen me all dressed up before at the club," Bailey smiled, taking a bite of her dessert, a salted caramel ganache with chocolate cake.

"The strip club don't count. It's nothing but smoke and mirrors in there."

"Oh you saying strippers are a bunch of frauds. Selling a fake fantasy," Bailey laughed.

"For the most part. But I don't have a problem wit' that. We all need an escape. I just like to see my women outside the club. Preferably in the daylight. Make sure I know what I'll be waking up to."

"So that means I've passed the daylight test."

"You wouldn't be sitting here at this table wit' me if you hadn't. If you haven't realized by now, I don't like wasting my time."

Bailey was joking when she made the comment to Rashan but she could tell by his response he was dead ass serious. The man was unapologetically arrogant. It made Bailey ask herself what did he see in her. She was about to ask him that very question until his driver approached and said something in his ear and then walked back over to his seat.

Rashan stood up suddenly. "I have to go. Chris will take you home."

"When will I see you again?" Bailey caught herself sounding disappointed, almost clingy.

"I'll be in touch. But go ahead and finish your dessert. Chris will wait for you." Rashan then tossed some money on the table for the bill and walked out.

When Bailey found herself wanting to chase behind him, she knew it was time to slow down and get her mind right. *Snap out of it Girl! This ain't a real date. You're on the job. He is your target and if Shiffon doesn't kill him then you will,* Bailey reminded herself.

"I thought Bailey would be home by now," Leila said to Essence, while flipping the channels trying to find something for them to watch on television. "Maybe I should call her."

"No don't do that." Shiffon objected, joining them in the living room. "If she hasn't come home that means she's still with Rashan. We don't want to give him any reason to start checking her phone."

"Do you think she's okay?" Essence questioned. "We haven't heard from her since this afternoon."

Just then, the women heard the front door opening and it was Bailey.

"There's our girl!" Leila smiled. "Look at you!" She stood up, greeting Bailey with a hug. "Last time we saw you, you were not wearing that dress."

"Sure wasn't," Essence said, admiring the white satin mini dress with a deep V neckline, front slit and knot detail cinching the waist.

"Yeah, Rashan took me shopping," Bailey said coyly. "We went out for dinner and of course I couldn't wear a jogging suit."

"Of course. Sit down and tell us more." Shiffon was ready to pick her cousin's brain. "But before you give us all the details, you didn't have Rashan drop you off here?" she wanted to confirm.

"No. Chris, Rashan's driver dropped me off at the address you gave me. The key was right where you said it would be. I made sure to wait until he was gone before I came here," Bailey told them.

"Great. Now spill it and don't leave anything out." Shiffon leaned forward as all the women listened intently.

"Well, he witnessed my epic fall at the club the other night and he didn't think I would be coming back to work. He was impressed with my resilience," Bailey giggled. "Oh and he's actually the owner of Privilege."

"Interesting and that also makes a lot of sense." Shiffon stated. "He's The King on the streets moving large quantity of drugs and Rashan when handling his legitimate businesses. Not too shabby...continue."

"Yeah, we got to talking and I ran with the background story you gave me Shiffon, struggling student who had to drop out of college and working at the strip club to get my money up. After we chatted for a while, he asked me to go home with him and of course I did."

"So you know where he lives...that's huge!" Shiffon's eyes widened with excitement.

"Don't get too enthusiastic. I don't think it's his main crib," Bailey shared.

"What makes you say that?" Leila was the first to ask.

"I mean there was nothing in there. It was completely furnished but it barely look lived in. I got the impression it was like a spot he just used..."

"To fuck women," Essence spoke up finishing the sentence for Bailey.

"Pretty much," Bailey agreed. "But I didn't fuck him," she wanted to make clear.

"Good! Because I don't need you falling in love."

"What is that supposed to mean, Shiffon?!" Bailey became defensive.

"It means exactly what I said. Men like Rashan are very charismatic and smart. They pull people in and have them become extremely loyal. How do you think they're able to rise that high on the totem pole and become a kingpin. You don't ever put your guard down when you're dealing with a man like that."

"I get what you're saying and I'll be careful," Bailey promised.

"So when are you gonna see him again?" Shiffon wanted to know.

"I'm not sure. We were having a really nice dinner and then his driver Chris came and told him something. Not sure what but whatever is was, Rashan bolted outta there."

"I'm almost positive it had something to do with two of Rashan's workers that Faizon had killed today," Shiffon shook her head.

"How do you know?" Bailey questioned.

"Because unfortunately I was there and saw the

shit with my own eyes. That's why I want us to finish this job and move the fuck on. Faizon rubs me the wrong way."

"I feel you but it's gonna take me a little time to figure out the best way for you to make your move on Rashan. The dude Chris is always with him and he has other security detail because they picked him up from the restaurant," Bailey divulged.

"I get it but we're closer to our goal now than we were a few days ago. Do you remember where Rashan's condo was?" Shiffon hoped her cousin could give her something, so she could start tracking her target.

"Yeah, better than that I saw some junk mail laying around and I made a mental note of the address and typed it in my phone. I was tempted to take a pic but then I figured a man like Rashan probably has cameras in his crib, even if it isn't his main spot."

"Very good, Bailey!" Shiffon clapped her hands with adoration. "Wise decision."

"I also wrote down the license plate number on his SUV." Bailey smiled proudly. "I told you I was taking my job seriously."

"Girl, you really showing out tonight!" Leila beamed, high fiving Bailey.

"This is excellent stuff. Bailey, text me over the info so I can have my guy run the plates. Until this job is finished I want you staying at that apartment. You never know when a man like Rashan might pop up. I want you to be there when he does. If you noticed, I got you a two bedroom. You ladies decide which one of you is going to be Bailey's aka Ayana's roommate. I don't want her staying alone," Shiffon told them.

"I think it should be Leila. I mean she is sleeping on the couch," Essence smirked.

"Thanks for your concern," Leila sneered. "But of course I'll be Bailey's roommate."

"Great, get your stuff together and head over to your temporary residence. Ladies, remember you're working. Stay on alert and watch each other's back," Shiffon emphasized.

"We're on it, boss!" Leila jumped up. "Now let me go pack my bags."

"I'll help you," Essence volunteered. "I wanna make sure you don't forget anything and have a reason to come back."

"You know you gon' miss me! Stop playing!" Leila teased, as they exited the room laughing.

"Bailey, are you sure you're good with this Rashan thing?" Shiffon asked her cousin once they were alone.

"You were just praising me, now you're doubting me...what gives?"

"When you were speaking about Rashan, I just got the impression you might've caught feelings."

"I don't even know him. How can I catch feelings." Bailey was trying to brush off Shiffon's assertion.

"We both know catching feelings for someone can happen in an instant. Men like Rashan are master manipulators. If you believe he is able to get inside your head mentally, then you need to tell me now, so you can back out. We can find another way to kill him."

"Shiffon, stop worrying. I got this." Bailey tried her best to reassure her cousin but deep down Shiffon wasn't convinced. Instead of following her gut instinct and shutting it down, she allowed Bailey to dance with danger.

Chapter Eight

TIME TO WALK AWAY

"If it ain't Ayana. Miss thang decided to bring her ass to work today," Dalia scoffed.

"Why do you have such a problem wit' me. Like I don't even know you." Bailey slammed her locker, rolling her eyes. "All I'm here to do is work and mind my business. I suggest you do the same."

"Are you threatening me?!" Dalia twisted her neck, coming towards Bailey.

"I'ma need you to step the fuck back before I put my foot up yo' ass. And if you think I won't...try me."

Bailey gave Dalia a menacing face, ready to scrap. She wasn't in the mood for the bullshit and was ready to brawl if need be. She wasn't the fighting type, as Bailey hated the idea of even breaking a nail but Dalia caught her on the wrong day.

"Girl, come on." Evte walked up grabbing Dalia's arm. "One of your customers out there asking for you. You tryna make money or be up in some bullshit?"

"You right. Ain't nothing in here worth seeing," Dalia snapped.

"Then carry yo' ass on then," Bailey popped back.

"Don't worry about Dalia," one of the other strippers came over to Bailey and said. "She just jealous because you the new girl and getting some attention. She always tryna scare somebody off. I'm Capri by the way," the petite beauty introduced herself.

"Ayana. How long have you been working here?"

"Since the place opened almost three years ago."

"I'm sure you've seen a lot of women come and go."

"Damn straight. Working in a strip club ain't for everybody. I'm here tryna make money to feed my daughter and take my ass home. Not here for all the shenanigans and extra drama but these chicks in here will try you, so beware," Capri cautioned.

"I will and thanks for the heads up. All I wanna do is work and make money too, just like you."

"Cool. I gotta go but I'll see you around," Capri said leaving out.

Bailey leaned back on her locker and let out a deep sigh. She had this anger boiling inside of her but it had nothing to do with Dalia, although she couldn't stand the broad. She hadn't heard from Rashan in almost a week. He stopped by the club last night but only stayed shortly and didn't say two words to her. Bailey began wondering had she said something to turn him off. She really wanted to go home and get in the bed because it wasn't like she enjoyed working at the strip club. Bailey was only there for Rashan and now it seemed as if he had lost all interest in her.

"Fuck! It's my turn to hit the stage," Bailey mumbled out loud when she heard her name being called out over the speakers.

Bailey strolled out in a golden metallic bootie short set with a slingshot and bikini bra top. She matched it with eight inch gold ankle strap sandals, decorated in multi size rhinestones studded on the tinted heel and outer side of the tinted platform bottom. Bailey was shining like a megastar but felt like shit. But as the track played, all the practicing she had been doing kicked in and she put that other bullshit behind her. Bailey knew Dalia and the rest of them fake ass hoes were watching, so she made sure to put on a show. And what better song to slide down the pole on than Cardi B's *Press*.

Press, press, press, press

Cardi don't need more press
Kill 'em all, put them hoes to rest
Walk in, bulletproof vest
Please tell me who she gon' check
Murder scene, Cardi made a mess
Pop up, guess who bitch?
Pop up, guess who bitch?

Ding dong!
Must be that whip that I ordered
And a new crib for my daughter
You know a bad bitch gon' spoil her
I got one in New York need one in Georgia
New Bentley truck cost a quarter
My money still long like weave
Pussy still wet like Florida
Everyone drop on the floor
She was talkin' but not anymore
MAC to your face like couture
This chopper come straight from Dior
Done with the talkin' I'm open to violence
Ask anybody they know I'm about it
Hashtag, #whipthathoass...

By the time Bailey finished her set, if all eyes won't on her when she hit the stage, they were as she made her exit, including Rashan. He had arrived at Privilege a few minutes before Bailey came out. As she was walking off the stage her eyes locked with his. Bailey was positive he was going to come over and speak to her but he didn't.

"You did all that gyrating and the nigga still don't want you. I guess you was a one and done." Dalia stood in Bailey's face and spewed. Bailey balled up her fist about to swing on her nemesis.

"Come on Ayana! Let's go get a drink." Capri quickly grabbed Bailey's arm, saving the day.

"The nerve of that bitch!" Bailey growled.

"Dalia ain't worth you losing your job and embarrassing yourself over. There's nothing cute about two strippers fighting in the club. You better than that," Capri said, handing Bailey a shot of tequila.

"Maybe but it sholl woulda felt good."

"Only for the moment. There's a strict policy here; no fighting on the floor. It's an automatic termination. If you must go to blows with Dalia, catch her ass in the locker room, or out in the streets," Capri advised.

"You right," Bailey agreed.

"Why does she have beef wit' you anyway...is it because of Rashan?"

"What makes you think it's because of him?"

"Last week I heard some of the girls talking and they mentioned they saw you leaving with him. You got they thongs in a mess," Capri laughed. "You know Rashan is the ultimate prize around here. They definitely don't want the new girl getting her hands on him."

"Well they don't have anything to worry about. Rashan isn't interested in me."

"You sound disappointed, which would be understandable. I mean the nigga is a great catch."

"Yeah so I heard. But I guess strippers aren't really his thing," Bailey shrugged.

"Maybe you're right. When Privilege had its grand opening a few years ago, Rashan brought his girlfriend. They seemed pretty serious. She used to come to the club with him a lot."

"Really...are they still together?"

"I don't think so. I haven't seen her here in almost a year now. Come to think of it, you all look kinda similar except she's definitely not a stripper. She has that real high maintenance look, with the attitude to match," Capri sulked.

"What do you mean?" Bailey was curious to hear her response.

"You know those chicks that think they better than everyone else because they man rich. All they wear are designer clothes, shoes, bags and walk around wit' they nose in the air. Well that's how she acted. Not sure what happened but they were definitely serious because if I'm not mistaken, I heard they were engaged at one time," Capri disclosed.

"Wow, they were serious." Bailey felt a twinge of jealousy and it made her uncomfortable.

Maybe Shiffon was right. I've caught feelings for Rashan but I don't want to admit it. I've been in a bad mood all week. I'm ready to scratch out his ex-fiancé's eyes and I've never even met the woman. All this jealousy and I haven't even kissed the man. Clearly I'm not thinking rationally. Yeah, it's time for me to walk away, Bailey decided.

"Hi Caleb. Thanks so much for coming all the way to Atlanta and meeting with me," Shiffon smiled, shaking his hand. "When Alex said you agreed to meet me here, I was very happy."

"Not a problem. I have to admit though, I wasn't expecting for you to look like you do." Caleb gave a slight laugh.

"Then we're both surprised because I wasn't expecting you to be so young. But I'm sure Alex told you I was a woman."

"No doubt but I wasn't thinking you was this type of woman. I mean you super feminine...real ladylike." Caleb remarked, observing her meticulously manicured long nails, the off white blazer mini dress that was the perfect mix of sexy and professional. And her makeup was soft yet accentuated her features flawlessly.

"I might look ladylike but the way I handle a weapon...there ain't nothing ladylike about it. I can promise you that." Shiffon got her point across.

"Based on how highly my man Alex speaks about

your services, I'ma believer."

"Glad to hear. Now tell me Caleb, what do you need for me to do?"

"I actually have two jobs. One is for myself in Philly and the other is for my boss Genesis. But I'll be your point person for both."

"That won't be a problem but it'll cost you a lot, plus a separate fee for incidentals and travel expenses."

"Money ain't an issue. I'll even throw in a bonus if you get shit done just right," Caleb grinned.

"We can start with a deposit but I'll be expecting my bonus too. Because I guarantee, you'll be pleased with our services," Shiffon stated with absolute confidence.

Chapter Nine

MY WAY OR NO WAY

"Girl, you been moping around here all day. What's going on with you?" Leila asked Bailey who was laying on the couch with a glass of wine in her hand.

"I'm fine, just debating if I'm going into work or not."

"Why wouldn't you go into work...you have a job to do." Leila gave Bailey the side eye.

"I still haven't heard from Rashan. The only reason I'm working at the strip club is to get close to him. There's no sense in showing up if he doesn't want me.

I don't feel like wasting my time," Bailey complained.

"You can't just give up. Why don't you call him. You have his number. We were hired to do a job, Bailey... remember."

"If Rashan wanted to speak to me, he would've called me by now, or spoke to me at the club. He hasn't said two words. It's like I've become invisible to him. I'm not about to play myself and call. I'm done with it. But stop worrying. Shiffon will figure out a way to deal with this mess, she always does."

"Stay right there," Leila said when she heard the doorbell. "We're gonna continue this conversation in just one second."

"There's nothing to talk about," Bailey pouted. She was too ashamed to confess to Leila, she was devastated that whatever interest Rashan had for her was now gone.

"Hi, can help you?" Leila asked the young man at the door who was holding a bouquet of flowers.

"Are you Ayana?" he asked.

"No, that's my roommate...are these flowers for her?"

"Yes."

"You can give them to me," Leila said, taking in the scent of the beautiful arrangement. "Where do I need to sign."

"Right here," he said handing Leila the paper. "But I'm not done yet. I have a whole van full of flowers for her."

"Are you serious?!" Leila smiled widely.

"Very. So if you can just keep the door open, I'll start bringing them in," the man said.

"Sure," Leila told him before calling out to Bailey. "Girl, come here! Look at all these flowers."

"These are for me?" Bailey's frown quickly turned to a smile. She ripped open the card that was attached.

I want to see you. I'll pick you up at 7. Be ready.

Rashan

"There from Rashan!" Bailey was extra giddy. She couldn't contain her excitement as the man filled up their entire apartment with the most exquisite flower arrangements.

"And yo' ass was over there on the couch whining, talking about he don't want you. Gotta give it to this Rashan dude. That nigga got class. You lucky bitch!" Leila laughed.

"I know! I need to go get dressed. He's picking me up at 7," she gushed as her eyes danced with delight.

"Girl yes. You go get ready. We need you to be looking super sexy for that nigga. Hopefully he'll take you to his main crib instead of that condo because Shiffon ain't got no movement at that spot," Leila said, following Bailey into her bedroom.

'That would be nice but I don't wanna seem pressed. Rashan strikes me as the type that doesn't like his women to be pushy."

"You probably right. I mean you didn't call him and look what it got you...a living room full of expensive ass flowers. Obviously you playing the game right. Keep at it baby girl!" Leila winked.

"Alright, now you can get out my room so I can get ready," Bailey giggled, shooing Leila out her bedroom and closing the door.

For the next couple hours Bailey spent her time getting all dolled up. This feeling of euphoria came over her, as if she was in high school again getting ready for prom. Instead of reminding herself that Rashan was a target, someone who was marked to kill, Bailey had drifted into dangerous territory. She no longer had control over her emotions, she had allowed herself to become vulnerable to a man she could never have.

"Hey, you ain't in here sleep, are you?" Shiffon asked, pushing Essence's bedroom door, that was cracked halfway open.

"Nope. Just laying down, flipping through this magazine. Why what's up?"

"I just sent Leila a text. She should be here in an hour or so. Tomorrow we're going to Philly for a couple days. It's a rather simple job that I think the three of us can handle since Bailey needs to stay here and work on Rashan."

"We got another gig...yes!" Essence hopped out the bed and cheered. "We need some cash flow up in here."

"I know, especially since Faizon's job is taking longer than I want it to. The address to the condo Bailey gave me, Rashan don't never be there. I had the tags ran and the car is registered to a corporation. This nigga just don't wanna be tracked. I hope Bailey is able to make some headway soon. But until then, we can't let the money stop. We got bills up in this muthafucka," Shiffon said, expressing her concerns to Essence.

"Who you telling...but umm, you not worried about leaving Bailey here? Maybe we should bring her with us." Essence suggested.

"It's only a couple days. What do you think can happen?"

"You know I ain't neva been one to hold my tongue, so I'ma just say it. I don't think Bailey cut out to handle a nigga like Rashan."

"And let me guess...you are," Shiffon said sarcastically. "You know damn well if you were in Bailey's position, you'd be all giddy over that nigga too."

"True but the difference is, I'd admit that shit. I wouldn't be tryna pretend he just another nigga. Bailey acting like she ain't infatuated wit' dude but it's obvious she is. I believe she's gonna end up getting her feelings hurt behind this shit," Essence reasoned.

"You might be right but anything that hurts you, can teach you. If Bailey allows herself to get emotionally attached to Rashan, eventually she'll have to admit it, learn from it and never repeat the shit again. Because we can't afford to let her fuck up twice."

"Did I tell you how beautiful those flowers were that you sent me," Bailey glanced over at Rashan and said.

"Yeah, at least a half a dozen times," Rashan replied, seeming preoccupied. "Chris, change of plans. Take us to Piedmont Park," he directed his driver.

"We're going to the park this time of night?" Bailey asked but instead of getting a response, Rashan ignored her.

We had this amazing dinner and now this nigga acting shady as hell. Oh fuck, did he find out the truth about me?! He ain't gonna take me to the park and kill me! Shit, should I text Shiffon, Bailey thought to herself, fidgeting with her iPhone. *I don't wanna die like this! Maybe I should just jump out the car and make a run for it.* Bailey put her hand on the door latch.

Then the car slowed down, turning down one of the most tranquil streets in the heart of Virginia Highland. Rashan's driver pulled up in the driveway of a modern contemporary house where Piedmont Park was basically the backyard of the home. A sense of relief came over Bailey. Rashan wasn't taking her to the park to kill her. He took her hand and led her inside his home.

"How many cribs do you have?" Bailey questioned, staring up at the 18' ceilings. She was greeted with Parisian stair-wrapped steel and glass, which was surrounded by an exposed concrete wall. The main living area had white oak flooring with an open concept that connected seamlessly into the formal dining room.

"In Atlanta or all over?" Rashan responded, placing his keys down. "Can I get you something to drink?"

"I'll take another glass of champagne, if you have some here."

"Of course I do. Relax, have a seat," Rashan said, disappearing into the kitchen.

"Your house is so beautiful," Bailey gushed. "I've never seen anything like it."

"I had it custom built. They only finished building it less than a year ago but I've rarely had time to stay here," Rashan said, coming back into the living room, handing Bailey the glass of champagne.

"Thank you." Bailey nervously sipped on her drink. Rashan had that effect on her. She found herself wanting to impress him but doubtful she'd measure up. "I thought you might mention it on your own but since you haven't, then I have to ask. I hadn't heard from you in over a week and you completely ignored me at the club...why?"

"I had a lot on my mind. There was a situation I

needed to deal with, that was business related. It put me in a bad mood. When I'm in a bad mood, I don't wanna be bothered."

"I see." Bailey swallowed hard. Rashan's bluntness always made her feel some kinda way. It made all her insecurities come to the surface.

"Is that a problem for you?" Rashan asked.

"No, it's not," she lied and said.

"Good because I wanna keep you around but only if you can fit into my life and that's not simple to do. I'm a complicated man, who lives a complicated lifestyle. I'm not easy to deal with."

"I already figured that out," Bailey giggled. "But I think it's one of the reasons I'm drawn to you. You're different than any man I've ever met."

"Yeah, I am. Now I need you to do something for me."

"What is it?"

"I want you to take off your clothes."

"You think because we've gone to a couple of fancy restaurants for dinner, you took me shopping and had a shitload of flowers delivered to my apartment, I'm just gonna have sex with you," Bailey balked.

"Who said anything about sex. I told you, I want you to take off your clothes. But if I wanna have sex with you, I will. And I won't have to force you, you'll willingly oblige."

Bailey was freaking out. Her stomach was doing somersaults. For a second, she felt a panic attack coming on. These gamut of emotions wasn't because she feared him but because she knew he was right. She had imagined her legs wrapped around Rashan as he thrusted in and out from the moment they first briefly locked eyes at Privilege. Bailey hated herself for wanting him and tried to deny it countless times but you can only lie to yourself for so long.

"I think it's time for me to go home," Bailey finally said, putting her glass down.

"Okay. I'll have Chris take you home." Rashan didn't protest, which only pushed Bailey to the verge of having a meltdown. She knew she needed to leave but she wanted Rashan to beg her to stay. Bailey stood up and grabbed her purse and walked towards the foyer. By the time she reached the door, she could feel Rashan standing behind her.

"I'll wait outside for Chris." Bailey turned around and said, looking up at Rashan whose deep dark eyes were once again pulling her in.

"I just sent him a text. He should be pulling the car around any moment," Rashan said, opening the door. Instead of walking out, Bailey hesitated. "Are you sure you wanna leave?"

"No...I mean yes I want to go," Bailey stuttered, wanting to turn away but feeling hypnotized by his stare. Almost like being under his spell. Rashan placed his hand under Bailey's chin and lifted her head up.

"Look me in my eyes and tell me that."

But Bailey couldn't. She tried to resist giving

into temptation but her desire for Rashan was much more powerful and he knew it. He had his hand on the nape of her neck and leaned down to kiss her. When Bailey didn't resist, Rashan became more aggressive. He began unbuttoning her blouse and pulling down her skirt. In a matter of minutes, she was standing in the foyer wearing only her bra, high cut lace Brazilian panty set and five inch heels, with Rashan's tongue down her throat the entire time.

"Why are you stopping?" Bailey questioned, breathing heavily when Rashan suddenly stopped the kissing and pushed her away.

"I said I wanted you to take off your clothes. Your clothes are off. Now I'm done."

"I don't understand. You kiss me, take off my clothes and then dismiss me!" Bailey screamed.

"Do you wanna be with me or not?" Bailey's eyes watered up. Her anger and humiliation wouldn't allow her to speak. "Answer my question." Rashan remained calm and unbothered by her reaction.

"Yes, I do," she conceded.

"Then next time I tell you to take your clothes off, you do it. I should never have to ask you twice. If you wanna be wit' me, that's the way it has to be. The choice is yours." Rashan stated before turning away.

"Where are you going?" Bailey called out.

"To bed. Now get dressed. Chris is outside ready to take you home."

Chapter Ten

I TOLD YOU SO

"Where the fuck is Leila!" Shiffon yelled out to Essence who was carrying her luggage down the stairs. "We're gonna miss our flight," she huffed, about to call her until Shiffon heard the front door open. "There you are! What took you so long...and Bailey what are you doing here?" she wanted to know, when she noticed her cousin walking in behind Leila.

"Sorry we're late but I had to pack," Bailey said putting down her suitcase.

"Pack for what?" Shiffon questioned, gathering the last of her belongings so they could go.

"I'm going to Philly with you all," Bailey announced.

Shiffon glanced over at Leila. "I mentioned our trip to her," Leila admitted. "I didn't think it was a big deal. She's part of Bad Bitches Only too."

"Yeah and Bailey needs to stay here and work on Rashan." Shiffon reminded her cousin. "The longer that job takes, the longer I have to deal with Faizon, which quite frankly I'm sick of. Aren't you supposed to be stripping tonight at Privilege? You can't be two places at one time, Bailey."

"I have a couple days off from the club and Rashan had to go out of town," Bailey lied. She just wanted to get out of Atlanta. After last night, the thought of having to face Rashan at work was too much. She didn't want to relive the embarrassment. "It makes no sense for me to stay here when I can help you with another job. Extra pair of eyes is always good."

"You have a point there but I didn't get a plane ticket for you and we need to leave asap," Shiffon stressed.

"No need to worry, I already bought my ticket and it's on the same flight. They had a few seats left," Bailey smiled, hoping her cousin would leave the issue alone and allow her to come to Philly with them.

"Alright ladies, then let's go!" Shiffon didn't have time to argue with Bailey. They had a job to do and money to make.

"You here early today," Malcom commented when Rashan came into the back office at Privilege.

"Yeah, I had something I needed to take care of. I was looking for one of the dancers...Ayana. Where is she?"

"Oh she called in and asked for a few days off. Said she had a family emergency and needed to go out of town," Malcom explained. "Why is something wrong?"

"Nah, I'll handle it. Thanks," Rashan said, leaving out the office and immediately calling her.

"Hello."

"Where are you?"

"On my way to the airport," Bailey said, making sure to tell everyone in the car to keep their voice down.

"Malcom said you had a family emergency and you weren't coming into work. What kind of emergency?"

"It was actually my roommate. She's dealing with some family issues and asked me to go out of town with her for support."

"So you lied." Rashan stated.

"I wouldn't call it a..."

"Go home now," Rashan demanded cutting Bailey off. I'll see you there in an hour."

"But..."

"But what?" Rashan cut her off again. "Didn't I tell

you last night, I should never have to ask you to do something twice."

"Yes."

"Then I'll see you in an hour and you better be there." And Rashan ended the call.

"What was that about?" Essence questioned when Bailey got off the phone.

"Rashan wants to meet me at the apartment in an hour."

"I thought you said he went out of town?" Shiffon inquired.

"There's been a change of plan."

"Then get you an Uber and have them pick you up at this IHOP," Shiffon said taking the next exit. "I would drop you off but we can't miss this flight."

"So what about me coming to Philly?" Bailey asked.

"What about it?" Shiffon retorted. "The only reason I was letting you come was because you said you didn't have to work and Rashan was going out of town. You have a job to do here. The three of us can handle Philly and you need to handle Rashan. Now order your Uber." Shiffon shut the conversation down, letting Bailey know this wasn't up for discussion.

Bailey wanted to beg Shiffon not to make her go back. Admit to her cousin she made a huge mistake being the bait to lure in Rashan because she was no match for him. Everything Shiffon claimed about him, was exactly on point but even worse. But Bailey didn't want to see the disappointment in her cousin's eyes or hear her say, I told you so.

"I'm doing it now," Bailey confirmed, typing in the where to information on the Uber App of her phone.

"Bailey, keep yo' game face on. Whatever you have to do, get close to Rashan. I'm ready for us to wrap this job up. I don't know how much longer I can tolerate Faizon. I'm so sick of that muthafucka," Shiffon seethed with a quiet rage. "The sooner you can set up the perfect opportunity for us to kill Rashan, the sooner we can close this case and collect the remaining balance of our money."

"I'll do everything I can," Bailey promised. "I'll see you guys when you get back from Philly," she said closing the car door and getting her luggage out the trunk.

"Kick ass roomie!" Leila yelled out the back passenger window.

"You all do the same!" As Bailey was waving goodbye her Uber was pulling up. "I know it said less than five minutes but damn that was fast," she said, when the driver blew his horn but she appreciated the quick arrival, especially since the traffic was already getting backed up. Bailey wanted to get to the apartment before Rashan. She preferred not being late but by the time she arrived, Bailey immediately noticed Chris in the driver's side of the silver Bentley Mulsanne and Rashan was in the backseat on the phone. She gave the Uber driver a cash tip and headed inside the apartment and poured herself a quick drink before Rashan came inside. She had to do something to stop herself from having an anxiety attack. Bailey quickly gulped down the rest of her wine when she heard Rashan knocking.

"I know you saw me in the car, so why did you lock the door?" was the first question out of Rashan's mouth when Bailey let him in.

"Habit, plus I noticed you were on the phone and I didn't know how long you'd be."

"So you were headed out of town and not gonna tell me," Rashan said, closing the door.

"After last night I didn't think you would care. You left me standing in the foyer half naked," Bailey said, pouring herself another glass of wine. "I don't even know why you showed up here. Is it to humiliate me again?"

"No." Rashan moved Bailey's hair over and placed his lips on the curve of her neck. He started with a gentle, soft kiss before sprinkling a few more. He slid the spaghetti strap to her floral flare mini dress down her arm and continued sprinkling kisses on her shoulder. When Rashan started to slide his hand up her inner thigh, Bailey wanted to tell him to stop but the warmth of his hand and the kisses had her aroused. He slid her panties to the side and caressed her clit before the finger fucking had Bailey about to have an orgasm.

"Don't do this again," she turned to Rashan and pleaded when he pulled away.

He put his finger to her mouth. "Shh." He flipped Bailey around and bent her over the island in the kitchen, lifted up her dress and ripped off her panties.

Rashan took his time gliding every inch of his dick inside the wetness of her pussy but with the thickness and length, Bailey was screaming out in pleasure and pain. She gripped her hands on the edge of the island, trying to endure each powerful thrust. When Bailey thought she couldn't take anymore, Rashan slowed down his strokes and pulled out. He laid her down on top of the island, spread her legs open and went from fucking Bailey with his dick to making love to her with his tongue. By the time he was done with her, Bailey was trembling as her orgasm shot through her entire body.

Chapter Eleven

MISSION COMPLETE

"You ladies ready for this?" Shiffon wanted confirmation from Leila and Essence, while making sure their guns were fully loaded.

"I'm good," Essence nodded.

"Me too," Leila agreed. "I'm excited! This my first hit busting shots."

"And lets not make it your last, so take this shit seriously," Shiffon advised. "Our main target is Mack but we want his crew too," she reminded them, showing a picture of the men together. "I'll be driving, so we in an out. I'll nod my head, when it's time to light them niggas up. I wanna make sure they close to the car because we can't miss our marks. Always think of your first chance, as your only chance. Now let's roll."

"Look at them bad ass bitches that just pulled up in the drop top beamer," Travis said to Mack as they stood outside in the parking lot of a popular nightclub. It was the thing to do every Thursday night and Mack was there with his crew front and center.

"You right. I ain't neva seen them around here neither. Some new blood," Mack chuckled. "We can be the first to break them in," he smirked.

"I want the one in the passenger seat. You know how much I love a pretty chocolate girl." Travis was already watering at the mouth, imagining how good Essence would look bent over with her ass up.

"Cool. I'll take the driver or the chick in the backseat." Mack decided.

"I'll take whoever left over," one of the other dudes spoke up and said.

"They look like they waiting on us." Mack licked his lips wishing he could fuck all three of them at the same damn time. The ladies looked like an early Christmas present sitting in their shiny ride. The only thing missing was a big bow.

"Ya gon' stand there or come talk to us?" Essence

called out in a seductive voice, from the front passenger side.

The guys didn't even try to play it cool. They came rushing towards the car full of eye candy like some dogs in heat.

"You ladies ready to go pop some bottles of bubbly or what," Travis offered.

"We have a better idea." Shiffon winked.

"Really, what's that?" Mack asked.

"We have an amazing present for you sexy mutherfuckas." Shiffon continued to tease.

"I love presents," one of the other dudes said.

"Me too." Mack nodded.

"Who wants their present first?" Leila questioned from the backseat.

"I do." Travis raised his hand.

"So be it." Shiffon gave the nod. "This present is courtesy of Caleb. Lights out niggas!" The women retrieved their heat simultaneously, catching the men off guard. All the guys were armed but because they were so busy thinking with their dicks, none of them were prepared to reach for their weapons in a time efficient manner.

"Oh shit!" Was all you heard the dudes say as the bullets came spraying, taking each of them down. Other patrons in the parking lot began screaming and scattering for cover. But the hit was so sweet and clean, it took the ladies less than two minutes to handle the job and be out without any repercussions.

Caleb watched in amusement as his hired shooters eliminated Mack and his crew with such ease. When their car sped away, leaving the dead bodies of his enemies, Caleb smiled, pleased with the outcome.

"Them chicks bad." Floyd grinned, looking over at Caleb who was sitting in the driver's seat. "Ain't nothin' like some sexy broads who can handle a gun. Them niggas didn't stand a chance."

"Sure didn't. Mack the one who wanted to go to war. I ended the shit before it could even get started."

"You did right, Caleb. As you like to say...always be proactive."

"You betta if you wanna win and stay alive in this game. And now that I got me some sharp shooters like them chicks...man I'm straight. I had my doubts. Fuckin' glad I listened to Alex. I'm keeping Bad Bitches Only on speed dial," Caleb grinned widely, pleased with their delivery.

Bailey hated it had to happen to her but within a matter of a few days, she'd become dickmatized by Rashan. He literally blew her mind and back out.

"Good morning," Bailey whispered in Rashan's ear before moving the sheet and going down on him. She started with the tip of his dick. Teasing it with her tongue. In seconds it came to life and was rock hard. When Rashan started moaning, Bailey knew he was pleased. He had spent the last couple of days training her to blow him just right.

"Damn," Rashan groaned, stroking her hair. "Your such a good girl. Now get on top." Bailey crawled on top and finessed up and down his tool like she was on the pole at the strip club. "Yeah, just like that," he said cupping her breasts, putting her hardened nipples in his mouth. Once Rashan felt her pussy throbbing and knew she was about to cum, he grasped the side of her hips, thrusting harder to go deep inside wanting them to cum at the exact same time. This was now their morning ritual.

"Every time you're inside of me, I wonder how I ever thought I had a great sex life before you," Bailey said, laying back down next to Rashan.

"I don't wanna hear about that shit."

"I only meant you're the best I ever had," Bailey clarified.

"I know what you meant and I don't care."

"Babe, I didn't mean to upset you."

"I know but you'll learn," Rashan said, reaching for his phone. "This has got to be the most consecutive days I've spent in this house and it's all cause of you." He leaned over and kissed Bailey. Rashan had this way of making her feel like a piece of shit but then in the very next second, have her believing she was special to him.

"I've loved spending this time with you but I know nothing last forever. It's time for me to get back to the club."

"That ain't happening."

"I don't understand. I told you last night Malcolm sent me a text saying I had to come in for work today."

"I haven't gotten around to calling Malcom but you're done at the club."

"Why?" Bailey regretted saying the word the moment it left her mouth.

"Because I said so. Do I need to give you a reason?"

"No of course not. But it's your club, so I was just surprised you didn't want me working there anymore."

Rashan caressed the side of Bailey's face and then firmly gripped her chin. "Do you think I would let the woman who's sleeping in my bed go shake her ass at the strip club in front of other niggas. Hmm? Answer me."

"No," Bailey shook her head. "It was a dumb question. I just wanna be near you. If I'm not working at the club, what am I supposed to do while you're gone?"

"Wait for me. As a matter of fact, you can stay here. It'll give me a reason to come home instead of staying at a hotel or one of my apartments."

"I'll stay but you have to make me a promise."

"I don't make promises." Rashan told Bailey. She put her head down but not before he caught a glimpse of sadness in her eyes. "I can't make any promises but tell me what you want."

"If I stay, I don't want you to get tired of me and make me leave."

Rashan stared at Bailey. She had this vulnerability that made him want to keep her by his side. "I've been around a lot of strippers but none of them have the openness you have. They have so many layers and built up walls. It's largely due to their love/hate relationship with men. They so damaged and the crazy part is most don't even know it. But you, I can still mold you. Make you what I need you to be to fit into life," Rasahn said, brushing back the hair covering the right side of Bailey's face. "Are you gonna let me teach you?"

"Yes. You can teach me." Bailey didn't waver. She wanted to please Rashan. Be everything he needed and more.

Chapter Twelve

NO GUIDANCE

"You know that nigga Rashan already brought in replacements for them workers we murked. They right back serving muthafuckas, killin' our profits," Tech raged to Faizon as they ate lunch in a hole in the wall restaurant Faizon owned in the Adamsville neighborhood, on the west side of Atlanta.

"Yeah, it's time for that nigga to go down. Muthafuckas out here callin' him The King and that shit done gon' to his head. Now he in these streets and think he untouchable." Faizon gritted his teeth.

"What up wit' ole' girl? I thought she was supposed to handle that nigga." Tech pushed his food away, losing his appetite.

"Yeah, I need answers. I'ma get 'em too." Faizon nodded towards the entrance of the restaurant.

"Didn't mean to interrupt your lunch but you said two o'clock and I like to be on time," Shiffon said when she got to the table Faizon and Tech were sitting at.

"It's all good. Have a seat. Tech, go put the closed sign up and lock the door," Faizon directed. "So what's up, Shiffon?"

"You tell me. You're the one who wanted to meet." Shiffon put the ball back in his court.

"How long is this Rashan shit gon' take? I figured this nigga be buried by now. Or at least his people would be making funeral arrangements."

"We both were aware taking down Rashan would not be easy. He ain't called The King for nothing."

"Fuck that nigga, he ain't no king!" Tech barked, taking his seat. "He bleed like everybody else."

"True. But just like it's harder to draw blood from some people's veins, others are harder to kill. It may not be fair but it's facts," Shiffon countered.

Tech was about to start popping off at the mouth again but Faizon pounded his hand on the table, signaling him to cut it out. "How much more time do you think this is gon' take? Rashan is fuckin' up my pockets. I kill his men, he bring mo' in. Like he got an endless supply of workers, which mean he makin' plenty of money. I gotta shut that shit down. Only way to do that is for you," Faizon pointed his finger at

Shiffon. "To kill The King."

"One of my girls has gotten very close to Rashan. We're in the planning stages of setting him up as we speak. He always has security detail with him and we also have to be careful to make sure not to get the young lady who works for me killed in the midst of taking Rashan down. We're very close to getting the job done. I just need you to be patient a little bit longer," Shiffon conveyed.

"Okay. I can do that. But Shiffon," Faizon's lanky body leaned forward. His bald head had a thin layer of perspiration, reflecting an extra shine. "My patience is wearing thin. I need that nigga dead. You understand?"

"Perfectly. Now can you unlock the door, so I can leave. I have work to do." Shiffon gave a gracious smile.

Faizon nodded at Tech who showed Shiffon to the door. "Man, I don't know about that broad. I think that bitch too pretty to kill any muthafuckin' body," Tech quipped after Shiffon left.

"She better deliver. Or it's gon' be her life on the line," Faizon asserted, finishing his food.

"What do you think of this?" Bailey held up the kiwi colored, deep v neck. long sleeve mini dress.

"It's super cute but a little bit more conservative than what you normally wear," Leila commented, browsing the aisle, trying to find her own outfit to wear.

"Rashan prefers more classy, sexy instead of too overtly racy. You know what I mean."

"Yeah I guess," Leila shrugged.

"What about this one? Rashan loves the color white on me," she smiled widely.

Leila stopped what she was doing and stared at Bailey. "Girl, everything out yo' mouth is Rashan this, Rashan that. It's like you can't make a simple decision without factoring Rashan in the equation. Are you in love with him?"

"You sound crazy!" Bailey tried to brush off Leila's interrogation. "I just wanna make sure I'm wearing the right dress to this party he's having. The goal is to make him trust me...right?"

"What the fuck does a dress have to do with a nigga trusting you?" Leila wasn't letting up.

"How is a fun day at the mall, doing some shopping, turn into you grilling me about Rashan? All I wanna do is find an outfit to wear to this party. So how did the gig in Philly go?" Bailey asked, wanting to switch the subject.

"Bailey, that shit was weeks ago."

"I know but we haven't really had a chance to talk since then."

"Yeah, because you been laid up under Rashan like he yo' husband. You haven't even been staying at the apartment."

"You haven't said anything to Shiffon have you?" Bailey wanted to know.

"No but only because she's been busy dealing with her own shit. Plus, I figured you were over at Rashan's crib working him but now I realize he's been working you," Leila snapped.

"You don't know what you're talking about."

"Not sure if you're in denial or what but I recognize when a bitch is dick whipped. Rashan completely has you open."

"Leila, can we just table this conversation for another time."

"Fine but you need to figure this shit out," Leila advised. "Falling in love with the man you're setting up to have killed, ain't never worked out in any woman's favor."

When Bailey got back to Rashan's house, after spending the day shopping with Leila, she was torn. She wanted to keep living in a fantasy world, that her and Rashan were in a real relationship and it was okay for them to be in love. But that wasn't reality and after the grilling Leila gave her, Bailey was starting to feel the walls close in on her.

"Did you find something to wear for the party?" Rashan questioned when Bailey entered the bedroom.

"Babe, I didn't realize you were home. I didn't see

Chris or the car out front."

"He'll be back shortly. I had him go pick something up for me right quick. Show me what you got."

"I got three different dresses. I hope you like at least one," Bailey said nervously, taking the clothes out of the shopping bags.

"Me too. I would hate to have to take you back to the mall," Rashan remarked, looking at what Bailey picked out.

"What do you think." Bailey stood off to the side, anxiously awaiting Rashan's input. She was like an eager child waiting for her father's approval.

"I like all three. You made some very good choices."

"Really?! I was worried you wouldn't like any of them. I didn't wanna disappoint you."

"You didn't," he assured her.

"Is there one dress you like more than the others?"

"The white one. It'll look perfect on you. Take off your clothes and try it on for me."

"Okay," Bailey said eagerly.

Rashan sat down on the cream chaise and watched Bailey take off the ribbed three piece set. She untied the belt on the sage duster cardigan, letting it fall to the floor. Next off was the matching bustier top and finally the wide leg pants.

"Don't move. Stand there for a moment. I wanna look at you." Bailey stood in the mesh, nude Demi balconnete bra and cheeky thong panty set with embroidery detail. "You got my dick so hard. Come kiss it for me."

Bailey walked over and got down on her knees. First, she slightly breathed on the frenulum-the tiny bump on the underside of his dick where the shaft meets the tip, right before her moist mouth made contact, tasting all of him. To keep Rashan stimulated, she gently massaged the perineum while giving him head. She alternated between longer ice-cream style licks with more traditional full-mouth over the dick sucking. Baily knew Rashan loved the idea of full dick sensation but his massive tool made deep throating impossible for her without gagging. So she wrapped her hand around the bottom of his shaft and took the rest in her mouth. She did it like that for a few minutes before placing the tip of her tongue on the roof of her mouth. Then letting his thick dick hit the underside of her tongue. Once Bailey felt the pulsating in her mouth she knew Rashan was about to cum.

"Baby, do you want me to swallow?" she asked after taking his dick out her mouth.

"Not this time," Rashan said, staring deep into Bailey's eyes while stroking her hair. "I'll just cum right there." He took his other hand and placed it on the cleavage of her breasts.

She went back to kissing, sucking, stroking and massaging Rashan's dick until he pulled it out her mouth and told her to lay down. He stood over Bailey and ejaculated all over her breasts and stomach.

"You look so sexy laying there." Rashan pulled up his pants, observing Bailey with lust in his eyes.

"Not as sexy as you, standing over me like that. I don't want you to put your dick away. I want it inside me. Please don't make me beg."

"I like when you beg." Rashan buttoned his pants and headed to the door.

"Baby, please come back. I wanna cum too. Pleeeeeease." Bailey had no shame in begging. "Rashan, where are you going? Don't leave me."

"I have to step out for a minute. If you're a good girl, I'll make you cum over and over again when I get back."

"You promise."

"You know I don't make promises but I got you. Until then, play with yourself and then take a shower. Make sure you ready for me when I get back."

Long after Rashan had left, Bailey was still laying on the marble floor staring up at the luxe crystal chandelier, gazing at the glass prisms. He hadn't been gone long but she already missed him. She missed the scent of his cologne, the smoothness of his chocolate skin and the defined muscles that sculpted his six feet two frame. Bailey began fantasizing about Rashan making love to her. She was about to start finger fucking herself, imagining it was Rashan but her phone wouldn't stop ringing and from the ringtone she knew it was Shiffon.

"Hello."

"Where are you?"

"At Rashan's house, so I really can't talk."

"I want you to come over tomorrow. We need to sit down and have a serious discussion."

"I can't come tomorrow. Remember Rashan is having a party, so I'll be busy all day and night."

"When you wake up Saturday, the first place you come after you brush your teeth is here. Are we clear?" Shiffon shouted.

"No need to yell. I can hear you," Bailey huffed.

"I'll take that as a yes. I'll see you Saturday."

"Fuck!" Bailey tossed her phone down on the bed. *Damn you Leila. You just couldn't keep your mouth shut. I can't worry about this bullshit right now. I'll deal with Shiffon later. All I wanna do is think about Rashan and him coming home to me,* Bailey thought to herself, going in the master bath to take a nice long hot bubble bath.

Chapter Thirteen

ACT UP

"Bitch, turn that shit up!" Dalia shouted to Tinaye as she was putting the finishing touches on her makeup before they left to head to the private party at Privilege. She rhymed to the City Girls track, grinding her hips to the beat, having her own pre-party.

I ain't got time for you fake ass hoes
Talkin' all loud in them fake ass clothes
Fake ass shoes match that fake ass gold
I'm the realest bitch ever to you snake ass hoes

Act up, you can get snatched up
Act up, you can get snatched up
Act up, you can get snatched up
Dirty ass nails, baby girl, you need to back up

It's Yung Miami, and I came to run my sack up
Tired ass hoes on my page tryna track us
Brand new chain, City Girls goin' platinum
I keep a baby Glock, I ain't fightin' with no
random, period...

"Girl, hurry up! We gotta go!" Tinaye screamed turning off the music.

"Why you turn my song off?"

"Because we ain't gon' neva leave this fuckin' apartment if I keep the music on. You over there dancing like we already at the club. I'm ready to go. You know traffic gonna be crazy. You always take too long," Tinaye criticized.

"Fine," Dalia smacked. "Let me finish puttin' on my lipstick. "Gotta make sure these lips look kissable. You know mad rich niggas gonna be up in that joint tonight."

"Who this party for again?"

"It's the three year anniversary party for Privilege. This my first year going because I missed it last year but Rashan been throwing one since first opening. I heard mad celebrities and ballers be there."

"Good, cause a bitch need a sponsor. I'm tired of workin' this nine to five, making chump change," Tinaye complained.

"I told you to come work at Privilege. We make some cute coins there." Dalia relayed to her friend.

"Girl, I'm too lazy to be up there shaking my ass. I just wanna perform for one nigga, not a club full on a daily basis. You can have that shit. I'm too bougie for all that mess." Tinaye flung her hair to side, grabbing her keys. "Come on, we got a party to attend."

"I knew you would look perfect in this." Rashan stood behind Bailey, staring at her reflection in the mirror. Admiring the white sparkling champagne sequin, backless dress. It had a mermaid silhouette that accentuated Bailey's curvy body like a second skin.

"Stop looking at me like that. When you do, I'm compelled to take my clothes off and beg you to fuck me."

"That'll have to wait. We need to go but before we leave, let me put this on you." Rashan took out a diamond necklace from the pocket of his suit jacket.

"Baby, you got this for me! It's gorgeous. When did you get it?" Bailey's eyes widened in disbelief.

"Yesterday, when I had to step out. I sent Chris to pick it up but there was a problem, so I had to go take care of it. I wanted to make sure it was perfect, just like you." Rashan sprinkled a kiss on Bailey's neck.

"Baby, it's flawless." Bailey glided her nail across the diamonds. "I don't deserve this and I don't deserve you."

"Why would you say that?"

"Because you have everything and I have nothing to offer you. I'm just an ex stripper."

"You're so much more than that. You have a lot of potential."

"Potential to do what?"

"Maybe you can go back to school," Rashan proposed. "I can pay for it of course."

"You would do that for me?" Bailey asked, full of guilt for lying to Rashan about her entire existence.

"Yes. I don't ever want you to think or say you have nothing to offer. If being here with me is not enough to make you feel good about yourself..."

"No! Rashan it's not that," she cut him off. "I feel like you're too good for me. I guess I'm scared one day you'll wake up and decide to replace me with someone else," Bailey admitted.

"How can I replace someone I'm molding to be my ideal woman. If you continue to listen and do as you're told, then you should become irreplaceable to me and that I can promise you."

"The man who never makes promises is making me a promise. Baby, I adore you." Bailey beamed, embracing Rashan with a long hug and kiss. She never wanted to let him go. Rashan was all she needed and more.

"Where the hell is Bailey!" Leila wondered out loud, standing by the bar with Essence.

"Who knows but we can't even mingle and enjoy ourselves. Shiffon made it clear, we're here to keep eyes on Bailey and Rashan."

"You mean babysit. I feel this job is taking forever to get done."

"That's because it is," Essence cracked. "If I didn't know better, I'd think Bailey is purposely prolonging this job, so she can keeping flirting with that fine ass nigga Rashan."

"Trust me she doing a lot more than flirting," Leila mumbled.

"I couldn't hear you...what did you say?" Essence questioned.

"I said, look who just walked in. Our girl Bailey, with her prince charming."

"Damn that muthafucka fine. Why couldn't my name have gotten picked." Essence shook her head, watching the couple go up to the VIP area.

"Should we go let her know we're here?"

"No. I mean Bailey knows we're coming but Shiffon said for us to monitor the situation from a distance."

"This should be a long and boring night."

"That's why we're posted near the bar. At least we can get a bit tipsy while we wait," Essence reasoned.

"Good point," Leila agreed, reaching over to get a napkin. "Fuck!"

"What happened?"

"I knocked my drink over and it spilled on my pants. I'll be back. I'ma go to the bathroom and try to clean this up," Leila said, grabbing her purse and heading to the ladies room. "Let me pee first," she said going into the empty stall.

"Bitch, you betta give that nigga yo' number," Dalia told Tinaye as they were coming into the bathroom.

"Girl, just because you think his watch is expensive, I'm supposed give out my number. That nigga mighta stole that shit. I need better receipts than just a watch to give up these digits," Tinaye popped.

"Whatever bitch. Speaking of bitches look who just walked in. If it ain't Miss Ayana."

"Why she look so familiar to me?" Tinaye asked.

'That's the chick we saw coming out of Phipps Plaza a while ago," Dalia reminded her friend.

"Don't come at me with that silly bullshit tonight." Bailey put her hand up, doing her best to ignore the foolishness.

"Oh, you think you that bitch, cause you went from stripping to fuckin' wit' Rashan. Trust me, in a couple months you gon' be right back on that pole wit' the rest of us."

"Tell them bitches wish, wish in my Cardi B voice," Bailey taunted the chicks.

"I remember where I know you from!" Tinaye belted. "We got in a fight a couple years ago at the mall over that nigga Dino."

"You must have me mistaken for somebody else." Bailey kept her poker face on but Tinaye wasn't budging.

"Nah, I remember that shit like it was yesterday. I just got my hair done. Paid all that money and you fucked up my weave."

"You sure, Tinaye?" Dalia frowned up her face. "You didn't mention that shit when we saw her at Phipps."

"We saw her from a distance and she wasn't all done up that day like she is now. Plus, I remember her voice. She was actin' all high and mighty because she thought she was Dino's girl. All while he was fuckin' wit' other bitches including me."

"Who is Dino?" Dalia was curious to know.

"He was a cute nigga, makin' some paper out in these streets. But he got murdered a few months ago. She was living wit' Dino when he got killed." Tinaye pointed her finger at Bailey.

"Like I said, I don't know a Dino and I ain't never got in a fight with you." Bailey was sticking to her story.

"Either you got a twin or you a muthafuckin' lie. But yo' name ain't no Ayana neither. It's something else."

Bailey could see the wheels turning in Tinaye's head as she tried to remember her real name.

"Tinaye, you sure about this shit?" Dalia pressed her friend.

"Fuck yeah. You think I'm not gonna remember a bitch I fought at the mall. As a matter of fact, I believe I still got a copy of the police report at home." Tinaye remained adamant.

"Ayana, or whatever yo' name is. Why you runnin' around using a fake name and shit? I knew there was something sneaky about you. Prancing around the club like you all sweet an innocent. You hiding something," Dalia nodded. "When my girl Tinaye get home, she gon' find that police report."

"Yep. I'ma find it alright. Cause yo' name damn sure ain't no Ayana." Tinaye could not be swayed. "There's no reason to lie."

"I know. That's why I didn't. But whatever. Like I said, I don't have time for the silliness. I have to get back to Rashan. You ladies enjoy your evening." Bailey glanced in the mirror and casually walked out.

"I can't stand that bitch but I think you might be wrong Tinaye," Dalia said, once Bailey left out the bathroom. "She was too cool, calm and collected. If the hoe was runnin' around here on some fraudulent shit, I think she woulda been more riled up," Dalia rationalized.

"I ain't gonna bullshit you. The bitch had me second guessing myself with how nonchalant she was. But if I'm right, she the best liar I done ever come across. I need her to hit the casino with me next time I play poker."

"Luckily, you still have that police report, so we'll find out when we get back to your apartment. I want you to be right because I would love to blow up her spot wit' Rashan. That nigga might think she a spy and kill her ass!" Dalia joked as she and Tinaye exited the bathroom laughing. She had no idea how close to the truth she was.

During the entire verbal altercation, Leila remained silent in the bathroom soaking in all the drama and it was nothing but bad for Bailey. She immediately got on her phone and called the one person who would know what to do.

"Shiffon, we have a serious problem..."

After her confrontation with Daila and Tinaye, Bailey couldn't bring herself to go back to the VIP area and face Rashan. She stepped outside to get some fresh air and calm her nerves. She felt pretty confident that she was convincing in her denials. But Bailey knew if Tinaye really did still have a copy of the police report, none of that mattered. Her cover would be blown.

"I thought that was you standing out here," the woman said, shaking Bailey out of her thoughts.

"I'm sorry, do I know you?" Bailey squinted her eyes at the unfamiliar face.

"No but we share a mutual friend."

"And who would that friend be?"

"Rashan. I'm Pilar. Rashan's ex fiancé." She reached out her hand to Bailey but she declined to shake it.

"I come in peace. There's no need to be rude, Ayana."

"I see you've done your homework and know my name. But not wanting to shake your hand doesn't make me rude," Bailey countered. "I have a lot on my mind and talking to my boyfriend's ex, isn't something I want to entertain right now."

"I heard you used to work here as a stripper," Pilar remarked, scrutinizing Bailey from head to toe. "That's where you met Rashan. But I don't get stripper vibes from you. Usually I can tell but you seem more polished. Unless Rashan just did an excellent job of cleaning you up."

"Obviously you're not gonna be easy to get rid of. So say your peace and let me be." Bailey was the one now doing the sizing up. She recalled how Capri described Rashan's ex and it was pretty much on point. Even her assessment that the two women had a very similar physical appearance.

"You're in love with him aren't you?"

"Excuse me!"

"The way you're so defensive. You're afraid of what I might say. You're worried and you have reason to be."

"Why is that, Pilar? I'm sure you're dying to tell me."

"Listen, I get it. You don't meet a man like Rashan very often. It can be intoxicating. The money, clothes, jewelry..." Pilar mentioned, unable to not notice the stunning diamonds decorating Bailey's neck. "And my goodness...the sex. He's still the best I've ever had."

"Can you get to the point." Bailey was losing her patience with the woman. She couldn't lie to herself though, there was a part of her that did want to hear what Pilar had to say. Who better to give her an insight into who Rashan was, than the woman he had planned on marrying at one time.

"It's easy to lose yourself and become consumed with being in Rashan's world. You'll be willing to do whatever it takes to please him but it will never be good enough. The moment you disappointment him, he will cut you off and not look back. He expects perfection, which doesn't exist in any woman. Prepare yourself and protect your heart. But that lovesick look in your eyes, I've seen it before. It used to be me, so I guess my warning came too late."

"There you are." Rashan came outside with two of his security detail. He appeared upset and ready to grill Bailey but then noticed the familiar face. "Pilar. I was told you were here. How are you?"

"As good as can be expected. I was out here getting to know your little friend better."

"You mean his girlfriend!" Bailey stepped close to Pilar and shouted. "And you weren't trying to get to know me better. You were trying to scare me off because you obviously still want Rashan for yourself."

Rashan had his hand on Bailey's wrist to contain her, as if he knew she was ready to strike. While keeping a steady gaze on Pilar.

"Your friend is being overly dramatic. I was only speaking the truth."

"You're so full of shit!" Bailey continued to yell. "You were basically stalking me and wouldn't leave me alone. Even though I made it clear, I wasn't interested in anything you had to say!"

Pilar stood there in her cognac colored, bandage jumpsuit, with her flawless hair and makeup, holding her designer bag, seemingly unfazed by Bailey's version of their interaction. But what happened next, left Rashan no time to gather all the facts.

"Boss, get down!" One of Rashan's security roared. The assailants drove up slowly in a late model gray Yukon Denali. The sudden and massive firepower left Rashan and his men overwhelmed. Armed with automatic weapons, the carnage came fast and furious. Shots kept ringing as the shooters relentlessly discharged bullets at their target. Rashan dropped to the ground, using his body to shield Bailey and Pilar. The front of the club was covered in bullet holes and the glass exterior shattered. As quickly as the murderous spree began it ended just as swiftly. The perpetrators fled the scene before law enforcement was able to respond, leaving a bloody massacre.

Chapter Fourteen

AFTERMATH

"I know you mad we left the party early but I couldn't focus on nothing else until I found out that bitch name!" Tinaye fumed to Dalia, while driving to her apartment.

"Well bitch I hope you right, cause I'ma be heated if we left for nothing," Dalia grunted, fidgeting around in her purse. "Stop at that corner store right quick, so I can buy some blunt wraps."

"Where you get some weed from?" Tinaye wanted to know, pulling up to the gas station.

"That dude I was talkin' to, that I fuck wit' sometimes. He gave me some smoke. He be having that official shit too."

"Well he better gave you enough for two cause we sharing that shit," Tinaye popped.

"You know I got you!" Dalia laughed.

"Bet! I'ma get some gas while you run into the store."

From a short distance Leila and Essence were parked in a raggedy old modeled car Leila had broken into and stolen. While Essence was keeping eyes on Tinaye and Dalia in the club, Leila was putting her hot wiring skills to use. Luckily, close to the vicinity she was able to quickly locate a car that was older than the mid-90s, as her method wouldn't work on newer models. Now here the women were waiting for the ideal opportunity to make their move.

"It's a good thing you were in that bathroom, heard them broads yapping and called Shiffon," Essence turned to Leila and said.

"I knew if anybody could come up with a plan and tell us how to execute it, it would be Shiffon. I guess that's why she's the boss."

"Bailey should've been the one making the call. She knew the chick had the police report and it would only be a matter of time before they found out her name definitely ain't no damn Ayana," Essence said, shaking her head.

"Okay, they on the move," Leila said, lifting her foot off the brake.

"Oh look!" Essence pointed in the direction of Tinaye's car. "They turned the wrong way and went down that alley. That's where we need to make our move. Go!"

Leila speeded up and made a sharp left turn into the alley right behind Tinaye's sportscar. She then slowed down. The women turned around to see who was behind them but were blinded by the excessive glare from the high beam headlights. Leila pressed down on the gas and slammed into the back of their car.

"What tha fuck is you doing! Move yo' shit and you bet not fucked up my car!" Tinaye hollered with fists bawled up and arms flaring.

Leila remained silent, stepping out the car and unloading three bullets into Tinaye. Putting two in the chest and one in the neck.

"Fuck is you doing?!" Dalia screamed out in fear seeing her friend murdered right in front of her eyes. She hopped in the drivers seat panic stricken. In haste to make her escape, Dalia mistakenly put the car in reverse and ran over Tinaye's dead body. She then switched gears to drive, hauling ass at a high speed. By the time Dalia realized there was a brick wall ahead, it was too late for her to slow down and she crashed, causing the airbag to deploy.

"You think she's dead?" Essence asked, looking over at Leila, who was standing next Tinaye's bloody and bruised body.

"Probably but go put two bullets in her head to make sure. Like Shiffon always tells us, never leave any witnesses."

"I'm on it." Essence sprinted to the car. There was a visible gash on Dalia's head but she was very much alive.

"Don't kill me...please," Dalia pleaded.

"Should've minded yo' fuckin' business!" Essence spit before putting two to the head.

"Boss you good!" Rashan's driver Chris and one of his bodyguards came running over.

"I'm fine."

"Ayana, are you alright?" Rashan was still on the ground with his arms around both women. It took Bailey a few seconds to realize he was talking to her as she was in a daze. "Ayana!" he called out again.

"Baby, I'm fine," she finally answered.

"Are you okay, Pilar?" Rashan turned his attention to his ex.

"Yes. I'm not hurt."

"Both of you stay...don't move. Let me check to make sure it's safe to get you outta here," Rashan said, standing up. There was at least half a dozen dead bodies sprawled in front of the club, including one of his security detail.

"I tried to catch up with the Denali but the driver turned down the street and I lost them for a minute. When I finally tracked it down, the truck was abandoned. They must've switched cars. But at least one of them was hit, because there was a lot of blood in the truck," Chris told Rashan.

"You get the word out on the streets, that I'm willing to pay whatever to find out who the fuck is responsible for this hit. I want all them muthafuckas dead."

"I'm on it boss!" Chris assured him.

Rashan then walked back over to Bailey and Pilar. "Chris is gonna take you home. I want you to stay at your place tonight. Better yet, I'll put you up in a hotel. Make sure you're safe," he told Bailey, who was still shaken up. "And Dennis will make sure you get home, Pilar."

"Rashan, I don't wanna leave you. Let me stay here with you," Bailey insisted.

"No and what did I tell you. Don't ever make me have to ask you to do what I want, more than once."

"After you're done here, will you come be with me at the hotel?"

"I don't know." Rashan stated firmly. "Right now, I want you to do as I say and let Chris take you to a hotel. I'll call you later." He gave Bailey a kiss and went back inside the club.

"I tried to tell you. Rashan is only going to let you in but so much. If you push too hard, he'll push away," Pilar walked over and said to Bailey once they were alone.

"Shut up! You let me worry about Rashan and

leave us the fuck alone!" Bailey seethed, storming off when she heard Chris calling her name. He was standing by the car, holding the door open for her.

Pilar had no intentions of leaving Rashan alone. Even if she couldn't get him back, she refused to allow him to move on with any other woman. In her mind, she truly believed no one understood the type of man Rashan was but her.

Chapter Fifteen

BLEEDING LOVE

"Do you know how fuckin' worried I was about you!" Shiffon screamed when Bailey showed up at their townhouse early the next morning, wearing the same dress she wore to the party last night.

"I didn't have my charger and my phone died. Rashan had me stay at a hotel and when I got there, I was completely exhausted and fell right to sleep," Bailey explained, flopping down on the couch. "Please tell me, you didn't have anything to do with that shooting at the club."

"Are you serious right now?! I freaked out when I heard about the shooting. I've been up all fuckin' night, scared you might've gotten shot and killed. Especially since the police are still not releasing any names of the victims. I can't believe you'd think I'd put your life in jeopardy and do a drive-by!" Shiffon barked.

"I'm sorry, Shiffon." Bailey put her head down. "I'm not thinking clearly right now. Everything is falling apart. This girl I used to work with at the club who hates me, is gonna find out, if she hasn't already, my real name. The first thing she's gonna do is run to Rashan!" She cried with fear in her eyes.

"Bailey, calm down." Shiffon sat next to her cousin and put her arm around her. "Don't worry. Dalia and Tinaye have been dealt with."

"How do you know about them?" Bailey wiped away the tears, surprised by what Shiffon divulged.

"I told you I was gonna have Leila and Essence there to keep eyes on you."

"I know but I didn't see them. I assumed they never came."

"That was the point. Watch you from a distance. If you saw them, it would've probably made you act differently in front of Rashan. I didn't want your behavior to make him become suspicious of you."

"Like always, you're the brains behind the operation. You get it right, when the rest of us get it wrong," Bailey sighed.

"None of that matters. What's important is you're alive and safe."

"When you say Dalia and Tinaye have been dealt

with, what exactly does that mean?" Bailey questioned.

"What do you think it means." Shiffon stood up getting her glass of juice off the table. "They're dead. Lucky for you, Leila happened to be in the bathroom stall when you had your altercation with them chicks," she said, taking a few sips.

"Wow!"

"Wow is right. Why didn't you call me immediately, Bailey?"

"I know I should've but I was worried about facing Rashan. Then I went outside to try and clear my head but Rashan's ex fiancée wouldn't stop harassing me. Next thing I know, Rashan comes out and all I hear is gunshots." Bailey's body tensed up and she spoke in a low voice. "I thought for sure Rashan was dead," she whispered, tearing up again.

"Have you forgotten that's what the end result is supposed to be...Rashan dead." Shiffon glared at her cousin intently. "I'm going to ask you a question, Bailey and I want you to tell me the truth. Are you in love with Rashan?"

Bailey couldn't bring herself to answer her cousin's question but she didn't have to. Shiffon could see it written all over her face. She paced the floor for a few minutes, weighing all their options but what Bailey said next left only one.

"I wouldn't ask you to do this for me unless I had to. Please don't kill Rashan!" Bailey begged. "I still have most of my share from the money you took from Dino. You can have it to pay back the deposit Faizon gave you. But I can't lose Rashan. I love him so much."

At this point the tears were pouring. Shiffon had never seen Bailey in this much pain before. Even with all the bullshit she went through in her tumultuous relationship with Dino, he never had Bailey fucked up in the head like this. It somewhat frightened her, the hold Rashan clearly had on her cousin.

"Bailey, are you sure this is what you want to do? I mean what do you think is gonna happen...you and Rashan will have this wonderful relationship and live happily ever after? How will you explain to him that you're not Ayana and that your real name is Bailey?"

"I'll figure it out. What's most important is that we have a chance to make it work. And the only way that's gonna happen is if you let him live."

"This is my fault," Shiffon huffed. "I knew it was too soon. After the hell Dino put you through, you weren't emotionally ready to deal with a man like Rashan. I should've insisted that either Leila or Essence be the bait."

"Shiffon, it isn't your fault. At this point, who cares. I'm in love with Rashan. I want a future with him. Please tell me you won't try to have him killed."

"I won't try to have him killed but you know Faizon isn't going to give up. He's probably behind the hit at the club. I told him about the party last night. Just so he would know we were working on the case and he would get off my back. Never did I think he would use the information to set up a drive-by," which pissed Shiffon off."

"You're probably right but I think Rashan can handle whatever Faizon brings his way. My only concern is you."

"Then you can stop worrying. I already have some other jobs set up. Being done with this means we can now move forward. I'll handle Faizon but I am gonna need that money."

"Of course. I want you to have it." Bailey stood up and walked over to Shiffon. "Thank you so, so much." She hugged her cousin tightly. "I will forever be indebted to you."

"Bailey, I need for you to be careful. Being with a man like Rashan can have you feeling like you're experiencing the ultimate high but all highs come crashing down. Some harder than others. Dino was a rookie compared to Rashan. I'll respect your decision but go into this relationship with your eyes wide open."

"Chino didn't make it," Tech informed Faizon when he got off the phone.

"Damn! Any word on Rashan?"

"Ain't nobody sayin' The King is dead, so I'm guessin' the nigga still alive."

"How is one muthafucka that hard to kill!" Frustrated, Faizon kicked over the chair. "The way the streets talk, it ain't gon' take long for Rashan to figure out I was behind the hit."

"I know and that nigga gon' be ready for war. What you wanna do?" Tech asked.

"Let's hope Shiffon and her crew have betta luck than us. I'll put some pressure on her. She need to kill that nigga before he seek retaliation. I'ma get her on the phone right now."

Faizon was more determined than ever to bring Rashan down and wanted him dead, by any means necessary.

Chapter Sixteen

YOU DECIDE

Bailey sat up in the bed watching Rashan sleep. Normally he was always the first to wake up but she had been tossing and turning, feeling restless. This was her first night back in Rashan's bed. Bailey assumed it would bring her comfort but it did the exact opposite. She was struggling to figure out how to come clean with Rashan without revealing all the details of her lies. But no matter how many different ways she tried to spin a plausible story, none of them made sense. She was deep into her thoughts until the vibration from Rashan's phone distracted her. She leaned over to see who was calling him so early in the morning and saw

Pilar's name on the screen. Unable to reach the phone without crawling over Rashan, Bailey jumped out of bed and grabbed his phone off the nightstand.

"What do you want, Pilar!" Bailey disappeared into the master bathroom, so Rashan couldn't hear her.

"Does Rashan know you're answering his phone? Of course not because he would never allow it."

"I told you to leave me and Rashan the fuck alone, now I'm warning you."

"Warning me? You think I'm scared of you, Ayana?" Pilar laughed.

"You should be." Bailey was consumed in her conversation with Pilar, she didn't hear Rashan get out the bed until he confronted her.

"Who are you talking to?" Rashan's voice startled Bailey. She turned around and saw him standing in the doorway.

"Pilar."

"Hang up the phone."

Bailey ended the call and handed the phone to Rashan. "I just wanted to know why she was calling you, especially this early in the morning."

"Then you ask me. Not answer my phone," Rashan said, going back into the bedroom.

"Then I'm asking you, what's going on between you and Pilar? Why all of a sudden has your ex fiancé reappeared in your life out the blue?"

"Pilar hasn't reappeared in my life, she never left."

"What does that mean?"

"It means even after we broke up, we've stayed in touch."

"Are you still sleeping with her?"

"No but if I was, would it matter?"

"Of course it matters! How can you even ask me that."

Rashan was sitting on the edge of the bed and Bailey knelt down on the floor between his legs, laying her head on the upper part of his muscular thigh.

"Why do you do this to yourself?" Rashan brushed his fingers through Bailey's hair, as if trying to console her. "Look at me."

She lifted her head up, staring at him. "How can you ask me would it matter?" Bailey had this glazed look in her eyes.

"If I told you I was still having sex with Pilar, you wouldn't stop seeing me. We would continue to be together, so why do you wanna drive yourself crazy. Look at you. You have tears coming out your eyes," Rashan said, wiping them away.

"But I love you."

"I know you do and that's why don't none of that other bullshit matter. You only gonna cause yourself unnecessary pain."

"Why did you and Pilar break up? And don't tell me it doesn't matter. I wanna know."

"Are you sure?"

"Yes! Tell me."

"I found out she stopped taking the pill and was tryna get pregnant."

"But you guys were engaged, why wouldn't you let her have your baby?"

"Pilar knew I didn't wanna get married or have any kids, so we compromised. We got engaged and agreed to get married and she agreed we wouldn't have any kids."

"Ever...you don't ever want kids?"

"Why would I wanna bring kids into this life I live. You see what happened at the club the other night. There's always a chance I can end up dead or in jail. Pilar knew how I felt but didn't care. I can't be wit' a woman I don't trust."

"I always imagined getting married and having a baby one day."

"I'm not gonna give you a baby. If having a child is that important to you, then I'll let you go." Rashan got up from the bed and opened the vast sliding glass doors that led out to the terrace.

Bailey joined Rashan outside. She stood behind him, placing her arms around his waist. "You know I can't let you go. You're enough for me. I don't need to have a baby. I'm happy just being with you."

"Pilar told me the same thing and it was a lie."

"Turn around and look at me," she told Rashan. "Do you think I'm lying to you?"

"At this very moment, of course you not lying. I know you believe what you're saying is true."

117

"Because it is. I'm not Pilar. I won't disappoint you." Bailey stood up on her tippy toes, placing a soft kiss on Rashan's lips.

Rashan lifted Bailey up and led her over to the outdoor sectional. He laid her body on the seat cushions and slipped off the sheer, soft sky colored, pleated chiffon babydoll teddy she was wearing. His tongue circled Bailey's hardened nipples and she bit down on her lip anticipating him filling up her insides. Rashan didn't disappointment. He knew she wasn't interested in the foreplay. Bailey wanted all of him inside of her. They made love outside on the terrace the entire morning until falling back to sleep in each other's arms.

"You got here fast," Faizon remarked when he opened the door to let Shiffon inside.

"How many of these rundown houses do you have?" Shiffon asked ready to leave the moment she arrived.

"Quite a few. The police have no interest coming to these neglected neighborhoods, which makes it easy for me to run my operation," Faizon explained, lighting a cigarette.

"I needed to speak with you, so it worked out when you called and said you wanted to see me." Shiffon wanted to get straight to the point and be out.

"It's good when we on the same page. I find shit be much more productive that way." Faizon continued puffing on his cigarette, sitting down on the one piece of furniture in the entire house. "I'm assuming you have an update regarding Rashan. You know I needed that nigga dead like yesterday."

"When I took this job, you told me The King would be difficult to kill. I underestimated just how accurate you were. But that didn't give you the right to use information I gave you, to orchestrate your own hit behind my back. You almost got one of my girls killed in that drive-by," Shiffon fussed.

"I admit, I was behind the drive-by but I was only tryna help you out," Faizon shrugged. "This doesn't change our arrangement. I can throw in a lil' extra for scaring yo' worker," he grinned smugly.

"Don't worry about it," Shiffon said, unzipping her purse. "Here's your deposit back." She placed the envelope of money next to him on the couch.

"What tha fuck you giving me this for." Faizon cut his eyes at the envelope and put his cigarette out on the armrest of the couch.

"I'm not gonna be able to finish the job. Even though we've put in a lot of time and resources, I'm willing to eat the financial loss and refund your money."

"I don't want the fuckin' money!" Faizon leaped off the couch, jaws flinching. "I hired you to do a job and you will finish it." He grabbed the envelope of money off the couch and threw it, hitting Shiffon in the chest.

Shiffon kept her cool not wanting to escalate an already tense encounter. Her only objective was to get out the house and away from Faizon.

"Listen, you can take the money or not take the money but I won't be doing the job. I'm sure you won't have any problem finding someone else. I wish you luck."

"Bitch, you ain't goin' no fuckin' where!" Faizon yanked Shiffon's arm as she was turning to leave. "I hired you to do a job and you gon' finish it!"

"Get yo' fuckin' hands off me!" Shiffon yanked her arm free. "Nigga, I don't work for you!"

"Oh yes the fuck you do!" Faizon wrapped his hand around Shiffon's throat and slammed her against the wall. "Unless you want me to fuck up that pretty face of yours, you done when I say so," he warned with nostrils flaring and spit flying.

Stay calm Shiffon. It's time to tap into what you've learned at those martial art classes you've been taking, she said to herself.

Shiffon took her left hand and held one of Faizon's arms with it. She then immediately took her right hand to strike his elbow joint with as much force as possible. Not letting up, Shiffon struck his neck, twisting his arm behind his back doing her best to dislocate it and shoving him to the wall, face first. Faizon managed to use his other arm to lunge a powerful punch to Shiffon's stomach. While struggling to catch her breath, he used the opportunity to reach for the gun in the back of his pants. Shiffon knew she had to quickly disarm him or risk being shot. She first, slightly moved her body to the side, so she wasn't directly in the line of fire. She then swung her purse to knock the gun out of Faizon's hand or at least distract him. With calculated swiftness, Shiffon kneed him in the groin, causing him to drop his weapon.

"I'ma kill you," Faizon moaned, throwing a sloppy punch that landed on the corner of Shiffon's mouth, busting her lip. Not getting sidetracked, she dived for the gun but Faizon latched onto her hair, yanking her head back. He balled up his fist, about to punch Shiffon in her nose. But before he could deliver the mighty blow, she dug her stiletto nails in his eye socket, causing him to damn near cry from the excruciating pain. It gave Shiffon just enough time to reach the weapon and without hesitation, she fired two shots to the dome. She knew he was good and dead but released one more shot because he had pissed her the fuck off.

Shiffon grabbed the envelope of money and hurried to clean up, making sure to leave no trace of her being there.

"Man, you won't believe the bullshit..." Tech stopped mid-sentence upon entering the house and seeing his boss laying in a pool of blood dead as Shiffon was coming out the kitchen. "I knew he shouldn't of trusted you!" Tech barked, reaching for his gun but Shiffon was quicker to the trigger, giving him no time to clap back. She kept shooting until there were no more bullets left. Shiffon grabbed her belongings and darted out the door before anyone else popped up without warning.

Chapter Seventeen

TRUE TO THE GAME

"I can't believe that dude Faizon fucked up yo' mouth like that! Piece of shit nigga!" Essence smacked.

"I'd rather be me with a busted lip than dead like him," Shiffon said, keeping some ice on her mouth, sitting on the sofa watching television.

"True but still, you didn't deserve to go through that bullshit. All this trouble because Bailey fell in love wit' some dick." Essence rolled her eyes.

"I think it's more than the great sex," Leila quipped. "I think she's genuinely in love with the man.

I hope it works out for them."

"Why am I not surprised," Essence said sarcastically.

"Faizon was a straight up asshole. What happened with him, isn't Bailey's fault."

"You always giving her a pass and being so protective of her," Essence shook her head.

"She is my cousin, plus I should've known better. It's not..."

"Shhh." Leila put her finger to her mouth, cutting Shiffon off. "Here comes Bailey."

"How was your nap, Bailey?" Shiffon asked, pretending they weren't just having a full conversation about her.

"It was good. There's nothing better than waking up next to Rashan but it felt nice sleeping in my own bed after all this time," Bailey smiled, sitting down next to her cousin.

"It's been nice having you here even if only temporarily," Leila smiled. "When are you going back to Rashan's place?" she asked.

"He should be home today, so I'm actually about to take a shower and get ready to leave shortly. I've missed him so much," Bailey admitted sweetly. "I know I've told you a million times but thanks so much for having my back, Shiffon."

"Always." Shiffon gently rubbed her cousin's shoulder.

"Yo! Turn the volume up!" Essence shouted, putting an end to the bonding moment between Bailey and Shiffon. Leila grabbed the remote off the table.

Breaking News...Local businessman Rashan Ellison has just been arrested at Hartsfield-Jackson Atlanta International Airport upon his return from Miami, Florida. Following a joint DEA/FBI investigation that spanned...

No one heard what the reporter said after that because Bailey fell off the sofa and passed out on the living room floor.

"Oh goodness! Is she gonna be okay?!" Leila screamed, running over to where Shiffon was. She was kneeling down, holding Bailey in her arms.

Essence went into the kitchen to get a bottle water from the refrigerator. She walked back into the living room and could see Bailey was starting to come to. "Give her this," she said handing Shiffon the water.

"Thanks."

"She still looks out of it!" Leila exclaimed.

"Bailey will be fine. She's just suffering from a broken heart and devastation. The kind that comes from not knowing when or if, she'll be able to hold and kiss the man she loves again." Essence reasoned. "It's one of the hazards of falling in love wit' a nigga like Rashan. Trust me, we've both been there," she sighed, looking over at Shiffon.

Shiffon knew Essence was correct but she hated it

had to happen to Bailey. After Clay and Bezo got locked up, both of them were struggling to get by. Not sure what to do with their lives. It was Bad Bitches Only that saved them. Shiffon couldn't help but contemplate what it would take to save Bailey from the pain of losing Rashan. But no one is immune to the pitfalls, of giving your heart to a man who is true to the game.

Epilogue

THREE MONTHS LATER...

The chauffeured drop top Maybach, slowly entered the gated, private, tree-lined driveway, set back on a magnificent custom 4 acre estate with lake views all around. The majestic grounds were truly breathtaking with strategic gardens, accent fountains, annexed terraces, heated in-ground pool, lighted tennis court, and a gazebo overlooking a stocked pond. The exclusive residence was located in Moorestown, NJ. Though it was only 15 miles from Philadelphia, it felt like an entirely different world. The beautiful suburb seamlessly married the modern with the past.

"Yo this crib is sick." Essence gasped.

"No doubt," Leila and Bailey both chimed in.

"I think we can all agree this is a beautiful estate but we're not here to drool over this man's crib," Shiffon quipped. "This is our highest paying gig so far. We cannot fuck it up. Are we clear?"

Shiffon made direct eye contact with each of the ladies. She wanted to make sure they were ready, especially Bailey, who had a rough last few months. When she finally spoke to Rashan, he said he was facing double digits in Federal Prison and was adamant she move on with her life. Bailey didn't care, she wanted to be there for him every step of the way, no matter what. Shortly after, he cut off all communication and she was devastated. She wouldn't come out her room and cried herself to sleep every night. It was a big step for Bailey to get back to work and Shiffon wanted to make sure her cousin was mentally prepared. She was about to find out.

The driver opened the back door and the four of them stepped out one by one, giving the appearance of a superstar girl group. The exquisite mahogany double doors opened and they were greeted with a, "Welcome. You can head straight to the back." The intimidatingly muscular bodyguard directed the women. After taking in the 3 story marble foyer and the grand center staircase, Shiffon noticed the gun toting goon, was armed with two Dan Wesson Valor 1911. But it was of no consequence to her, he was on the payroll.

"Ladies, let's go," Shiffon glanced back signaling her girls. All you heard was the clicking of their designer heels, on the Calacatta marble floor until they reached the archway.

"Well, I be muthafuckin' damned," Trae gasped, laying his playing cards down. He didn't care he'd exposed his hand. Imagining the fun he was about to have with the eye candy standing in front of him, was worth the few thousand dollars he'd inevitably lost on the card game.

"Nigga, what you doing?!" Eli, another player at the table scoffed. It didn't take long for him and the other men in the room, to see what had garnered Trae's full attention.

"Maverick told me he had hired some prime pussy but man oh man, them hoes are exceptional," another player chimed in and said.

"Speaking of Maverick, here come that nigga now," Trae said, as he was stepping off the glass elevator.

"You already know this, but you the man, Maverick!" Eli and the other men in the room cheered.

"That must mean my special invited guests have arrived," Maverick smiled widely.

"Damn straight," Trae nodded.

"No need to stand over there. Come sit down and join us," Maverick said, walking over to the women and taking Shiffon's hand. "Would you ladies like some champagne?" he offered, pointing towards a table stocked with bottles of expensive bubbly.

"We'll be more than happy to sit down and have a drink, after you hand over our money," Shiffon stated sweetly. Although she nor the other women had any intentions of drinking.

"A woman about her business. I like that," Maverick remarked. He went over to a desk in the corner of the room, opened the drawer, retrieved some money and placed the stacks in Shiffon's hand. 'This is the amount we agreed on, plus a little extra."

"Thank you," she said, placing the money in her bag. Shiffon then turned to Essence, Bailey and Leila letting them know it was time to get to work.

The women wasted no time, taking off their Gucci G-Sequence print coats. They removed the belt on their classic silk blend trenches revealing La Perla lingerie and Dita Von Teese lace, mesh curve enhancing bodysuits.

"Gotdamn!" The men belted, seeing nothing but toned, glistening flesh.

The DJ who was hired for what was supposed to be a small birthday celebration for Klay, one of Maverick's top workers, turned the music up to get the party on ten. Cardi B's Drip featuring the Migos started blaring from the surround sound speakers, which automatically got the women hyped, to start doing what they do best...perform.

With tits and ass grinding seductively in their faces, the men were losing it. "I need you to come closer," Trae demanded, groping Bailey's thigh. His hand was itching to slide her panties to the side and get his fingers drenched in her wetness.

"What about me?" Maverick asked Shiffon with ease, while they sat watching all the pussy poppin' and lustful glares from the other side of the room.

"I was waiting for your request." Shiffon stood up, releasing her trench. As if having no impulse control, Maverick reached out and ran his hand down her bare stomach.

"You have the most beautiful skin. It's fuckin' soft too," Maverick continued, working his hand down her leg like he was mesmerized. "Why the fuck you strippin'? You supposed to be some nigga's wife."

Not replying with words, Shiffon straddled Maverick while arching her back. She placed his hands on her breasts and allowed him to cup them tightly. Unable to resist the temptation of seeing her hardened nipples, Maverick slid the lace fabric on the bra to the side. The ladies were hired to strictly dance but Shiffon had his dick so hard, he was willing to pay top dollar so they could fuck too.

"What I gotta do to have you?" Maverick moaned.

"I'm yours, daddy," Shiffon teased, before placing her nipple in his mouth. She immediately felt his dick fighting to come out his pants. Maverick kissed, licked and sucked, gripping her waist firmly not wanting to let her go.

Shiffon caressed his face, purring and moaning,

feeding into Maverick's desires. With the music bla-ring, intoxicated off her body, her scent, her touch, his mind was in another world, leaving him powerless.

"You have to be mine," he mumbled. It wasn't until the sharp needle pressed through his neck, did Maverick realize he had been set up.

"Genesis sent me," Shiffon whispered to Maverick, with a deadly glare in her eyes, making sure the full dosage of the clear liquid drug trickled in his blood stream. But the first few drops were so potent, it had rendered his body paralyzed. Maverick was unable to move or speak, yet his mind was completely alert.

The notorious, yet lowkey drug kingpin, had to watch in silence as the beauty he'd instantly become infatuated with, took out his crew. Shiffon's weapon of choice was a needle for Maverick but she came with gun's blazing for his team. Eli was the first to get it. He had a bottle of champagne in one hand and gripping Leila's ass with the other. He felt zero pain as the bullet ripped through his brain.

Once Eli went down, the domino effect was in full swing. The ladies had murder on their mind and made sure to stay sober, while the men were too drunk to realize death had shown up at the front door. Leila, Bailey and Essence retrieved guns from their trench coats, that was conveniently draped on the chair they were giving lap dances on. Trae, Klay, a couple of other men and even the DJ, who wasn't a member of Maverick's crew, were all shot dead within a matter of seconds, as Cardi B's Invasion Of Privacy continued to blast in the background.

"You all take whatever you like but keep an eye on Maverick. I'll be right back," Shiffon told her girls after checking to make sure the intended targets were deceased.

"I was wondering what was taking you so long," the muscular bodyguard who let them in said, as Shiffon walked towards him.

"I wanted time for my girl's to put on a proper show and have the liquor circulating correctly, before we put in the real work," Shiffon winked.

"Least them niggas died wit' a smile on they faces," he chuckled.

"I'm sure they did," Shiffon smirked, reaching in her purse. "Here's your cut for staying out the way."

"Thank you," he grinned, eyeing his stacks of dead presidents.

"My pleasure. I'm about to get our driver, so he can put Maverick in the trunk. Do you wanna take your bullet in the shoulder, leg, arm....it's up to you."

"I'll take it in the arm. All these muscles will protect me," he joked.

"Cool, now hand me your guns. We want to keep this as realistic as possible. We need it to appear you were taken out. Not that you willingly let us kill everyone here and kidnap your boss."

"True," he nodded. "I already gave your driver the video footage. There's nothing to show you all coming or going," he stated, handing her his weapons.

"Perfect." Shiffon nodded, before using one of his own guns, to put two bullets in his head. "Sorry, but I can't afford to leave any witnesses," she shrugged, grabbing the money she'd just given him, from his closed fist.

Shiffon opened the front door, signaling for the driver to come inside. As far as she was concerned, their job was done and it was time for them to make their exit. Unbeknownst to Shiffon, this wouldn't be her last encounter with Maverick. In fact, he would be the one to change her life forever.

Coming Soon...

A KING PRODUCTION

Stackin' PAPER

a novel

JOY DEJA KING

Chapter One
A Killer Is Born

Philly, 1993

"Please, Daquan, don't hit me again!" the young mother screamed, covering her face in defense mode. She hurriedly pushed herself away from her predator, sliding her body on the cold hardwood floor.

"Bitch, get yo' ass back over here!" he barked, grabbing her matted black hair and dragging her into the kitchen. He reached for the hot skillet from the top of the oven, and you could hear the oil popping underneath the fried chicken his wife had been cooking right before he came home. "Didn't I tell you to have my food ready on the table when I came home?"

"I... I... I was almost finished, but you came home early," Teresa stuttered, "Ouch!" she yelled as her neck damn near snapped when Daquan gripped her hair even tighter.

"I don't want to hear your fuckin' excuses. That's what yo' problem is. You so damn hard headed and neva want to listen. But like they say, a hard head make fo' a soft ass. You gon' learn to listen to me."

"Please, please, Daquan, don't do this! Let me finish frying your chicken and I'll never do this again. Your food will be ready and on the table everyday on time. I promise!"

"I'm tired of hearing your damn excuses."

"Bang!" was all you heard as the hot skillet came crashing down on Teresa's head. The hot oil splashed up in the air, and if Daquan hadn't moved forward and turned his head, his face would've been saturated with the grease.

But Teresa wasn't so lucky, as the burning oil grazed her hands, as they were protecting her face and part of her thigh.

After belting out in pain from the grease, she then noticed blood trickling down from the open gash on the side of her forehead. But it didn't stop there. Daquan then put the skillet down and began kicking Teresa in her ribs and back like she was a diseased infected dog that had just bitten him.

"Yo', Pops, leave moms alone! Why you always got to do this? It ain't never no peace when you come in this house." Genesis stood in the kitchen entrance with his fists clenched and panting like a bull. He had grown sick and tired of watching his father beat his mother down almost every single day. At the age of eleven he had seen his mother receive more ass whippings than hugs or any indication of love.

"Boy, who the fuck you talkin' to? You betta get yo' ass back in your room and stay the hell outta of grown people's business."

"Genesis, listen to your father. I'll be alright. Now go

back to your room," his mother pleaded.

Genesis just stood there unable to move, watching his mother and feeling helpless. The blood was now covering her white nightgown and she was covering her midsection, obviously in pain trying to protect the baby that was growing inside of her. He was in a trance, not knowing what to do to make the madness stop. But he was quickly brought back to reality when he felt his jaw almost crack from the punch his father landed on the side of his face.

"I ain't gon' tell you again. Get yo' ass back in your room! And don't come out until I tell you to! Now go!" Daquan didn't even wait to let his only son go back to his room. He immediately went over to Teresa and picked up where he left off, punishing her body with punches and kicks. He seemed oblivious to the fact that not only was he killing her, but also he was killing his unborn child right before his son's eyes.

A tear streamed down Genesis's face as he tried to reflect on one happy time he had with his dad, but he went blank. There were no happy times. From the first moment he could remember, his dad was a monster.

All Genesis remembered starting from the age of three was the constant beat downs his mother endured for no reason. If his dad's clothes weren't ironed just right, then a blow to the face. If the volume of the television was too loud, then a jab here. And, God forbid, if the small, two-bedroom apartment in the drug-infested building they lived in wasn't spotless, a nuclear bomb would explode in the form of Daquan. But the crazy part was, no matter how clean their apartment was or how good the food was cooked and his clothes being ironed just right, it was never good enough. Daquan would bust in the door, drunk or high, full of anger, ready to take out all his frustration out on his wife. The dead end jobs, being broke, living in the drug infested and violent prone city of Philadelphia had turned the already troubled man into poison to his whole family.

"Daddy, leave my mom alone," Genesis said in a calm, unemotional tone. Daquan kept striking Teresa as if he didn't hear his son. "I'm not gonna to tell you again. Leave my mom alone." This time Daquan heard his son's warning but seemed unfazed.

"I guess that swollen jaw wasn't enough for you. You dying to get that ass beat." Daquan looked down at a now black and blue Teresa who seemed to be about to take her last breath. "You keep yo' ass right here, while I teach our son a lesson." Teresa reached her hand out with the little strength she had left trying to save her son. But she quickly realized it was too late. The sins of the parents had now falling upon their child.

"Get away from my mother. I want you to leave and don't ever come back."

Daquan was so caught up in the lashing he had been putting on his wife that he didn't even notice Genesis retrieving the gun he left on the kitchen counter until he had it raised and pointed in his direction. "Lil' fuck, you un lost yo' damn mind! You gon' make me beat you with the tip of my gun."

Daquan reached his hand out to grab the gun out of Genesis's hand, and when he moved his leg forward, it would be the last step he'd ever take in his life. The single shot fired ripped through Daquan's heart and he collapsed on the kitchen floor, dying instantly.

Genesis was frozen and his mother began crying hysterically.

"Oh dear God!" Teresa moaned, trying to gasp for air. "Oh, Genesis baby, what have you done?" She stared at Daquan, who laid face up with his eyes wide open in shock. He died not believing until it was too late that his own son would be the one to take him out this world.

It wasn't until they heard the pounding on the front door that Genesis snapped back to the severity of the situation at hand.

"Is everything alright in there?" they heard the older lady from across the hall ask.

Genesis walked to the door still gripping the .380-caliber semi-automatic. He opened the door and said in a serene voice, "No, Ms. Johnson, everything is *not* alright. I just killed my father."

****

Two months later, Teresa cried as she watched her son being taking away to spend a minimum of two years in a juvenile facility in Pemberton, New Jersey.

Although it was obvious by the bruises on both Teresa and Genesis that he acted in self defense, the judge felt that the young boy having to live with the guilt of murdering his own father wasn't punishment enough. He concluded that if Genesis didn't get a hard wake up call, he would be headed on a path of self destruction. He first ordered him to stay at the juvenile facility until he was eighteen. But after pleas from his mother, neighbors and his teacher, who testified that Genesis had the ability to accomplish whatever he wanted in life because of how smart and gifted he was, the judge reduced it to two years, but only if he demonstrated excellent behavior during his time there. Those two years turned into four and four turned into seven. At the age of eighteen when Genesis was finally released he was no longer a young boy, he was now a criminal minded man.